LESBIAN
EROTIC
STORIES
& POETRY

More Serious Pleasure

Edited by the Sheba Collective

Published in the United States by Cleis Press Inc., P.O. Box 8933, Pittsburgh, Pennsylvania 15221, and P.O. Box 14684, San Francisco, California 94114.

Originally published in England by Sheba.

Printed in the United States.
Cover design: Ellen Toomey
Cover photograph: Jill Posener
Logo art: Juana Alicia

Library of Congress Cataloging-in-Publication Data

More serious pleasure : lesbian erotic stories and poetry / edited by the Sheba Collective.
p. cm.
ISBN: 0-939416-48-4 (cloth) : $24.95. — ISBN: 0-939416-47-6 (trade paper) : $9.95
1. Lesbians—Literary collections. 2. Women—Sexual behavior—Literary collections. 3. Lesbians' writings, American. 4. Lesbians' writings, English. 5. Erotic literature, American. 6. Erotic literature, English. I. Sheba Collective.
PS509.L47M67 1991 91-2575
810.8'0353—dc20 CIP

First Edition.
10 9 8 7 6 5 4 3 2 1
ISBN: 0-939416-48-4 cloth
ISBN: 0-939416-47-6 paper

Grateful acknowledgment is made to the following for permission to reprint previously published material: "Eat" by Sapphire was first published in *Women on Women*, eds. Joan Nestle and Naomi Holoch, and is reprinted with the permission of New American Library. "Piece of Time" by Jewelle Gomez first appeared in *On Our Backs*.

CONTENTS

INTRODUCTION

In May 1989 Sheba published *Serious Pleasure: Lesbian Erotic Stories and Poetry,* edited by the collective. It was a British first, and as such we felt it necessary to write a comprehensive introduction. We wanted to situate ourselves and the book within the context of the times: both in the wider society and in relation to the ongoing lesbian feminist debates and sometimes bitter arguments around the meaning of erotica.

Serious Pleasure was an overnight success: going into reprint within the first two months. It was clear to us that such a contextualized introduction seemed unnecessary for *MORE SERIOUS PLEASURE.* It was evident that our readers liked the stories — a second volume had to be published! We were excited and pleased by the numbers of women who wanted to read erotic stories which represented the wide diversity and variety of our sexual lives and fantasies. Our call for stories resulted in another deluge. We were delighted! *MORE SERIOUS PLEASURE* was underway.

MORE SERIOUS PLEASURE is exactly that. Interestingly, however, in such a short time, many of the stories are significantly different from those we printed only a year ago. Not only did lesbian writers want to write about sex, this time round they seemed eager and able to develop sustained story lines and interesting plots. Never fear, there is still a mix of straightforward sexual encounters and sexual fantasies. As we said in our introduction to *Serious*

Pleasure, 'We do not expect every lesbian to like, approve of, or be driven to having sex by every story in this book.' The same holds true for *MORE SERIOUS PLEASURE.*

There is still no feminist consensus about the difference, if any, between erotica and pornography, let alone what a feminist definition of pornography is. Sheba is a feminist publishing house, collectively run by a racially mixed group of women; we have built our reputation around a passionate commitment to women, to open and critical debate, to a recognition of the differences between women, and to change now and in the future. Both *Serious Pleasure* and *MORE SERIOUS PLEASURE* are a part of that passionate commitment, which is shared with all the other titles we publish every year.

In *Serious Pleasure* we also included a section on lesbian safer sex. Only one story actually referred to safer sex. Largely the same is true in *MORE SERIOUS PLEASURE.* However, we still believe that lesbians should 'think long and hard about HIV and AIDS and seriously take on the hows and whys of safer sex.' We refer readers to the safer sex notes in *Serious Pleasure* and urge them to talk about safer sex with their partners. We are still interested in reading more lesbian safer sex stories and exploring the reasons, if any, why safer sex is not reflected more in the fiction lesbians write.

Ultimately, we hope you will read and enjoy, again. Until the next time ....

The Sheba Collective
London,
July 1990

PIECE OF TIME

JEWELLE GOMEZ

Ella kneeled down to reach behind the toilet. Her pink cotton skirt pulled tight around her brown thighs. Her skin already glistened with sweat from the morning sun and her labour. She moved quickly through the hotel room sanitizing tropical mildew and banishing sand. Each morning our eyes met in the mirror just as she wiped down the tiles and I raised my arms in a last wake-up stretch. I always imagined that her gaze flickered over my body; enjoying my broad, brown shoulders or catching a glance of my plum brown nipples as the African cloth I wrapped myself in dropped away to the floor. For a moment I imagined the pristine hardness of the bathroom tiles at my back and her damp skin pressed against mine.

'Okay, it's finished here.' Ella said as she folded the cleaning rag and hung it under the sink. She turned around and as always, seemed surprised that I was still watching her. Her eyes were light brown and didn't quite hide their smile, her hair was dark and pulled back, tied in a ribbon. It hung lightly on her neck the way that straightened hair does. My own was in short tight braids that brushed my shoulders; a coloured bead at the end of each. It was a trendy affectation I'd indulged in for my vacation. I smiled. She smiled back. On a trip filled with so much music, laughter and smiles, hers was the one that my eyes looked for each morning. She gathered the towels from the floor and in the same motion opened the hotel room door.

'Goodbye'.

'See ya.' I said, feeling about twelve years old instead of thirty. She shut the door softly behind her and I listened to the clicking of her silver bangle bracelets as she walked around the verandah toward the stairs. My room was the last one on the second level facing the beach. Her bangles brushed the painted wood railing as she went down then through the tiny courtyard and into the front office.

I dropped my cloth to the floor and stepped into my bathing suit. I planned to swim for hours and lie in the sun reading and sip margueritas until I could do nothing but sleep and maybe dream of Ella.

One day turned into another. Each was closer to my return to work and the city. I did not miss the city nor did I dread returning. But here, it was as if time did not move. I could prolong any pleasure until I had my fill. The luxury of it was something from a fantasy in my childhood. The island was a tiny neighborhood gone to sea. The music of the language, the fresh smells and deep colours all enveloped me. I clung to the bosom of this place. All else disappeared.

In the morning, too early for her to begin work in the rooms, Ella passed below in the courtyard carrying a bag of laundry. She deposited the bundle in a bin, then returned. I called down to her, my voice whispering in the cool, private morning air. She looked up and I raised my cup of tea in invitation. As she turned in from the beach end of the courtyard I prepared another cup.

We stood together at the door, she more out than in. We talked about the fishing and the rain storm of two days ago and how we'd spent Christmas.

Soon she said, 'I'd better be getting to my rooms.'

'I'm going to swim this morning,' I said.

'Then I'll be coming in now, all right?'

'I'll do the linen,' she said, and began to strip the bed. I went into the bathroom and turned on the shower.

When I stepped out the bed was fresh and the covers snapped firmly around the corners. The sand was swept from the floor tiles back outside and our tea cups put away. I knelt to rinse the tub.

'No, I can do that. I'll do it, please.'

She came toward me, a look of alarm on her face. I laughed. She reached for the cleaning rag in my hand as I bent over the suds, then she laughed too. As I kneeled on the edge of the tub, my cloth came unwrapped and fell in. We both tried to retrieve it from the draining. My feet slid on the wet tile and I sat down on the floor with a thud.

'Are you hurt?' she said, holding my cloth in one hand, reaching out to me with the other. She looked only into my eyes. Her hand was soft and firm on my shoulder as she knelt down. I watched the line of the muscles in her forearm, then traced the soft inside with my hand. She exhaled slowly. I felt her warm breath as she bent closer to me. I pulled her down and pressed my mouth to hers. My tongue pushed between her teeth as fiercely as my hand on her skin was gentle.

Her arms encircled my shoulders. We lay back on the tiles, her body atop mine, then she removed her cotton t-shirt. Her brown breasts were nestled insistently against me. I raised my leg between hers. The moistness that matted the hair there dampened my leg. Her body moved in a brisk and demanding rhythm.

I wondered quickly if the door was locked. Then was sure it was. I heard Ella call my name for the first time. I stopped her with my lips. Her hips were searching, pushing toward their goal. Ella's mouth on mine was sweet and full with hungers of its own.

Her right hand held the back of my neck and her left hand found its way between my thighs brushing the hair and flesh softly at first, then playing over the outer edges. She found my clit and began moving back and forth. A gasp escaped my mouth and I opened my legs wider. Her middle finger slipped past the soft outer lips and entered me so gently at first I didn't feel it. Then she pushed inside and I felt the dams burst. I opened my mouth and tried to swallow my scream of pleasure. Ella's tongue filled me and sucked up my joy. We lay still for a moment, our breathing and the seagulls the only sounds. Then she pulled herself up.

'Miss ...' she started.

I cut her off again, this time my fingers to her lips, 'I think it's okay if you stop calling me Miss!'

'Carolyn,' she said softly then covered my mouth with hers again. We kissed for moments that wrapped around us making time have no meaning. Then she rose. 'It gets late, you know,' she said with a giggle. Then pulled away, her determination not yielding to my need. 'I have my work, girl. Not tonight, I see my boyfriend on Wednesdays. I better go. I'll see you later.'

And she was out the door. I lay still on the tile floor and listened to her bangles as she ran down the stairs.

Later on the beach my skin still tingled and the sun pushed my temperature higher. I stretched out on the deck chair with my eyes closed. I felt her mouth, her hands and the sun on me and came again.

Ella arrived each morning. There were only five left. She tapped lightly, then entered. I would look up from the small table where I'd prepared tea. She sat and we sipped slowly; then slipped into the bed. We made love, sometimes gently, other times with a roughness resembling the waves that crashed the sea wall below.

We talked of her boyfriend, who was married and saw her only once or twice a week. She worked at two jobs, saving money to buy land, maybe on this island or her home island. We were the same age, and although my life seemed to already contain the material things she was still striving for, it was I who felt rootless and undirected.

We talked of our families, hers so dependent on her help, mine so estranged from me; of growing up, the path that led us to the same but different place. She loved this island. I did too. She could stay. I could not.

On the third morning of the five I said, 'You could visit me, come to the city for a vacation or ...'

'And what I'm goin' to do there?'

I was angry but not sure at whom: at her for refusing to drop eveything and take a chance; at myself for not accepting the sea that existed between us, or just at the blindness of the circumstance.

I felt narrow and self-indulgent in my desire for her. An ugly, black American, everything I'd always despised. Yet I wanted her, somehow, somewhere it was right that we should be together.

On the last night after packing I sat up with a bottle of wine listening to the waves beneath my window and the tourist voices from the courtyard. Ella tapped at my door as I was thinking of going to bed. When I opened it she came inside quickly and thrust an envelope and a small gift-wrapped box into my hand.

'Can't stay, you know. He waiting down there. I'll be back in the morning.' Then she ran out and down the stairs before I could respond.

Early in the morning she entered with her key. I was awake but lying still. She was out of her clothes and beside me in a moment.

—

Our lovemaking began abruptly but built slowly. We touched each part of our bodies imprinting memories on our fingertips.

'I don't want to leave you.' I whispered.

'You're not leaving me. My heart go with you, just I must stay here.'

Then ... 'Maybe you'll write to me. Maybe you'll come back too.'

I started to speak but she quieted me.

'Don't make promises now, girl. We make love.'

Her hands on me and inside of me pushed the city away. My mouth eagerly drew in the flavours of her body. Under my touch the sounds she made were of ocean waves, rhythmic and wild. We slept for only a few moments before it was time for her to dress and go on with her chores.

'I'll come back to ride with you to the airport?' she said with a small question mark at the end.

'Yes,' I said, pleased.

In the waiting room she talked lightly as we sat: stories of her mother and sisters; questions about mine. We never mentioned the city nor tomorrow morning.

When she kissed my cheek she whispered, 'sister-love' in my ear, so softly I wasn't sure I'd heard it until I looked in her eyes. I held her close for only a minute, wanting more, knowing this would be enough for the moment. I boarded the plane and time began to move again.

MATERIAL GIRLS

SPIKE PITTSBERG

Looping the knot on her slender black leather tie, Berry unconsciously rounded her back and rolled her shoulders forward, so as to reduce the folds her tits imposed on her white silk shirt when she inadvertently stood straight. The smell of brilliantine on her hair bothered her, so she grabbed her bottle of Old Spice, spilled some into her hands, and ran them through her Duck's Ass. As she brought her face close to the mirror, she felt the usual conflict: put on mascara or not? She loved mascara, had always loved it, but found her attachment to it slightly perverse and inappropriate. 'Fuck it,' she thought to herself, 'I'm too old for this bullshit. Anyway, who's gonna be able to tell in a darkened club?' Once her lashes were blackened, she realized — in a daily ritual that had been going on for twenty-five years — why she liked the stuff. '*Now* you are looking good,' she complimented her image.

◆ ◆ ◆

Vera wished that someone were around to help her tighten up her corset laces. The pinkish-yellow satin corset was one of her many undergarments frequently worn but rarely seen. Vera wore them because of what they helped her turn into. She liked having her soft breasts grasped and raised by the firm slinky material, liked having her rib cage secretly hugged the night long, and particularly appreciated the encouragement the pinched waist gave her to stand tall, shoulders back, ass projected. Vera struggled into the lycra leotard. She had to tug hard in order to snap the two ends together in her crotch, but the effort was well-spent. She had purposefully bought it a size too small, liking the sturdy ceaseless caress it provided between her legs.

◆ ◆ ◆

Berry drew on her grey tweed wool slacks and her cashmere sports jacket. She jerked her white cuffs so that they stuck out evenly from her coat sleeves. Tucking the ends of her shirt collar under her lapels, she tried to decide whether or not to add a hanky in the breast pocket. 'Better not,' she said to herself, 'it'll look too much like an obvious effort.' With a final buff to her cowboy boots, she went out the door of her apartment.

◆ ◆ ◆

Vera zipped up her black leather skirt, which together with her pointy black ankle boots completed her outfit. Her hair was even wilder than usual, kinky, luxurious masses of darkness around her long thin-featured face. As she put on her deep red lipstick, she had a flash of nostalgia for the white lipstick of her teen years. She remembered the first time a woman had eaten off the white colour along with the greasy lip gloss she used to apply, but quickly recalled herself to the present. The girls would be by within minutes to pick her up for the drive to the club, and they'd kill her if she was late yet again.

◆ ◆ ◆

Berry parked her 10-speed across the street from the bar and while leisurely locking it up, watched the various combinations of women going in the door. It was a trendy crowd tonight, and young, she noted, but then that was to be expected with the kind of group that was performing. 'The Cuff of My Hands' was a Dutch band out of the Amsterdam s/m scene. They had got their start jamming in a gay squat bar, and this was their first international tour. There were a lot of titillating rumours about their act.

◆ ◆ ◆

'Oh, there's a spot,' Vera cried, pointing ahead to a car pulling out of a precious parking spot. Her friend at the wheel immediately sped up to the place, and everyone's mood improved. They had been driving around for a quarter of an hour, while make-up melted, clothes stuck to the back of well-dressed thighs, gel hardened, and tensions grew. 'Good work, Vera!' they congratulated her. 'You should take this as a good omen: your eyes are sharp tonight!' They piled out, laughing with happy expectation, and entered the club.

Standing in line at the ticket office with her buddies, Vera absently studied the back of the woman in front of her. She noted the fine cashmere of the jacket, the shimmering hair iced back into a DA, and the smartly creased slacks. Still flushed by her success in finding them a parking place, she felt a sudden curiousity to see the front of this woman.

'Excuse me,' she said breathlessly, leaning over the woman's shoulder and noting with mild disappointment that she was shorter than herself, 'How much are they taking for tonight's tickets?'

Berry turned only her head, and that only a few inches. 'Triple the usual, naturally.'

Dissatisfied, Vera tried again. 'Yeah, but I heard that "Cuff of My Hands" is worth any price.'

'Why? Do you know anyone who has ever actually seen

them?' Berry asked out of the side of her face, and then turned around to get her answer.

The two women looked at each other, Vera with anticipation, and Berry with welcome surprise.

'Wow,' the butch thought, 'so not everyone tonight is gonna be an androgynous young punkster.' The woman behind her in line was outrageous. Her hair looked like it had some Hollywood wind-blowing machine secreted inside its abundance; her face was at the same time tight and pouty, dazzling, witch-like; but the rest of her was hidden by an ankle-length dark blue overcoat that fell in thick folds from super-padded shoulders.

Vera had been asked a question. 'Uh, no. I haven't seen them, I mean no one I know has, but I read a long review of them last week ...' At that point the cashier called, 'Next please' and the woman in front of her turned to move up, pulling an alligator wallet out of her back pocket. Vera had only had time for a quick impression, but she certainly liked what she saw. 'Maybe I am gonna have luck tonight,' she thought, noting the woman's big eyes, and the mascara which emphasized them.

By the time she and her friends bought their tickets, she had lost sight of the woman. Peeved, she began to move into the main room, only to be stopped by a hand thrust out from inside the doorway.

'Berry,' the butch said. Shaking the hand, she answered, 'Vera. Nice to meet you.'

'So you were saying ... about the review?'

They chatted for a few minutes, but Vera's friends soon came to take her to the bar to order drinks. Just as they were served, the band came onstage and their group pressed to get close. The four band members sported various degrees of shaved heads with the odd braid or coloured tuft sprouting out of their scalps. They were dressed in the obligatory plethora of leather and chains and belts and high-heels. Their music was harsh, their stance hostile, and their act peculiar. The first few songs were accompanied by screams and screeching and it was hard to catch the point. By the fourth song, the lead singer was standing next to the drummer, who was making music with one hand, and unsnapping the singer's vest with the other. The drummer pulled out the singer's generous tit and began pulling on it vigourously. She kneaded the flesh roughly, then focused on the nipple, which she pinched between her thumb and forefinger, all the time never missing a beat.

'Reminds me of a mammography,' Vera heard in her ear. And she turned around to face Berry. She laughed, relieved to know that someone else in the crowd was less than thrilled by the band's act, and happy that Berry had found her.

Since it was impossible to talk in the din, the two were satisfied to just stand next to each other watching the show. During an instrumental number, the lead singer danced over behind the bass player, who spread her legs widely apart, stretching her denim mini-skirt taut, while balancing herself on exaggerated spike heels. The singer sat herself on the floor between the bass player's legs and began rubbing the woman's calves and thighs. Slowly working her way upwards, her hands disappeared into the woman's crotch, the view of which was blocked from the audience's sight by the oversized bass. But the movement was unmistakable. Vera and Berry could see the motion of the singer's upper arm and elbow, prodding upward to the pulse of the music. The bass player's eyes closed, her head dropped forward, her legs seemed to tremble, but she stuck to her playing.

As the singer became more spirited, helping the bass player to stay erect with one hand on her ass, and fucking her with the other, the rhythm of the song picked up, faster and faster. The audience could feel the degree to which the bass player was exercising her powers of concentration and self-control, as her arms continued to function on her instrument, while the rest of her was responding to the singer's hand. The bass player began to plunge into a near squat, harder and faster, and the audience jerked slightly along with her. The tension grew and grew and Vera felt herself backing up slightly, so that her overcoat was brushing Berry. Berry noticed the movement, leaned her weight a bit forward on her toes, and made the contact explicit. Just then the song reached its peak, ended with a crash, and the lights blacked out on the stage.

The crowd was silent for a couple of breathless moments, and then completely broke up in cheers, clapping, and whistling. Vera relaxed backward onto Berry who stepped forward with one leg between Vera's for support, and they remained in a quiet tingle as everyone around them began to mill about.

The emcee came on to thank the 'Cuff of My Hands', and to announce the beginning of the disco. A 'Fine Young Cannibals' song flooded out of the sound system, and the atmosphere was defused. Vera turned towards Berry, took a step away, and smiled. Berry indicatd with a twist of her head, and the two of them walked towards the back room, which was set up with tables and chairs.

Before they sat down at a corner table, Berry went behind Vera and said, 'Aren't you hot in that coat? Let me help you off with it.' Vera unbuttoned the tiny blue buttons, and Berry eased it down her shoulders. The lycra leotard flashed black, disappearing into the shining black leather skirt. Berry could not resist putting her hands on Vera's shoulders and turning her gently around to face her. The plain approval evident on Berry's face gave Vera the courage to go with this thing. It had been a long long time since she had last considered acting on one of her frequent attractions. She had been burned too often, and rather badly at the end of her last affair. Since then her flirtations had remained just that: flirtations.

Berry strode around to her own side of the table and they stared at each other a second before sitting down simultaneously.

'How very slender she is,' Berry thought, 'under those blown-up shoulder pads and those mounds of hair. How fucking striking she is!'

'She likes me,' Vera thought, 'Do I like her?' She noted the impeccable silk shirt closed with the matt leather tie, but she couldn't see much more than that since Berry was encased in the armour of her sportscoat.

They talked as dykes do, about the show and the crowd at first, then about themselves, their jobs, their apartments. They shared some humous and pita and drank black coffee, and then Vera asked Berry to dance. Making their way back into the main room, Berry took her hand, and both of them were startled and happy at this first touch.

When a slow number finally came on, Vera rested her arms on Berry's shoulders, while Berry's arms went around her tiny waist. 'I wish I wasn't so damn short,' Berry thought, as she had a hundred times in her life. By imperceptible degrees, she held the beautiful woman closer and closer, thrilled to find that Vera followed her old two-step easily. At the end of the number, they remained entwined, still on the dance floor, and Berry turned up her head to say into Vera's ear, 'Let's go be alone.'

Vera pulled back gently to look at her, wondering to herself, 'It's been so long. Maybe this is a mistake ...', but Berry already had her hand and was heading back to the table to get Vera's coat.

'I, uh, have to tell my friends that I'm leaving,' she said, 'I'll meet you outside in a minute.'

Her friends were wise enough not to make a big deal out of what they knew to be a very unusual development in Vera's life. She took a deep breath and headed outside.

'I've got my bike here,' Berry told her. 'Either we can leave it here and take a cab, or walk it back together. I mean, if you'd like to come over to my place, that is. It's less than a mile from here.'

'Ah, a brief reprieve,' Vera thought. And out loud said, 'Yes, it's not raining. Let's walk.'

For awhile they were quiet, and then Berry told her, 'Listen Vera, I don't wanna go into all the gory details, but I want you to know that I haven't been with anyone, at least not very seriously, for long years. I'm a bit uptight right now. Just wanted you to know.'

Unexpectedly, Vera burst out laughing. 'God, lesbians!' she nearly choked. 'I was just about to tell you the same thing.'

'Really?' Berry was amazed. 'You've been single for awhile?'

'Awhile? That's not the word for it. I've been alone for three years.'

'Far out! I mean, not far out for you, but, I don't know, it makes things more equal or something.'

Once inside her one-room apartment, the two women fell silent over cups of hot tea. Both felt that something potentially serious was coming down, and both felt a simultaneous resistance and attraction. Berry, sensing Vera's ambivalence, left the first move up to her. Eventually Vera moved over to Berry, turning her face openly towards her. Berry put both hands on the sides of Vera's head, covering the woman's ears, and drew that fascinating face towards her. Vera felt that suddenly the whole world had been expelled; she could hear only the heat from Berry's hands. Berry pulled Vera's lips onto her own unmoving ones, and they met in a dry soft still first contact. They stayed that way, until pressure from Berry's hands brought Vera's face closer. Still dry, still soft, but not so pristine.

They broke away slightly, just far enough to look at each other, and then Berry moved one hand to behind Vera's neck, again pulling her forward. This time Vera's tongue went out, to gently wet her own and Berry's lips. The next kiss spelled commitment, as they both opened their mouths, sucking on each other's tongues, rolling their lips in among and around each others', hugging close. They moved over to the bed, still kissing, and Berry sat Vera down on her lap. Instantly Berry felt enfolded, surrounded, absorbed into the reams of wavy hair that showered down from Vera above her. It was like being inside a sweet-smelling wispy tent of exciting filaments. Without thinking, she fell backwards, Vera falling with her, on her, for her.

Soon their hands were running over cashmere, lycra, leather, silk. As Vera eased off Berry's jacket, Berry unloosened her tie. Kicking off her own boots, she then jumped down off the bed to remove Vera's. For the first time she saw the sexy woman's stockings, the old-fashioned grey silk type, the seam a dark line running up from the heel and disappearing invitingly at the back of her thighs under her skirt. Berry, squatting at the foot of the bed, couldn't restrain herself from running her hands up and down Vera's calves and knees. Her senses could barely distinguish between the silk stockings and the woman's skin, and touching her with her hands was no longer enough. She grasped the woman's feet against her own chest and rubbed the silk feet against her silk-shirted tits. Vera's toes clutched at her shirt, at her breasts; both women began getting very excited.

Leaning forward with her arms encircling the other woman's thighs, Berry slid her chest up and down Vera's legs. It was as if her nipples, like fingertips, were exploring the length of Vera's legs.

'Come back,' Vera appealed quietly, and Berry quickly mounted the bed. She turned Vera onto her stomach and unzipped the tight skirt. She returned to the foot of the bed to ease off the pliant black material from Vera's legs, catching sight of Vera's garter belt. 'Oh my god,' escaped her lips on a heavy exhalation of breath, causing Vera to pick up her head to look at her. The garter belt was pink. lacey, outrageous, and Berry felt herself getting wet at the sight. Vera sat up, unsnapped her leotard and swiftly removed it over her head. She was the ideal which Frederick's of Hollywood never had the class to achieve. Berry saw her laced pink corset, her breasts pushed up aggressively over the top; and below, the pink garter belt reaching out from Vera's waist in four tendrils, past her naked pussy and ass. Berry had never had such a visual sexual high; the breath was knocked out of her.

Vera used the pause to both cover her own embarrassment, and to strip her new lover. She unbuttoned the silk shirt, revealing small low breasts at the opening, slipped the tie over Berry's head, and worked on her cuff-links. 'Cuff-links!' Vera thought to herself. 'We're both like a flash from the past.' Berry stood to remove her own slacks, keeping her eyes locked on Vera's face. Vera scooted down to the edge of the bed, to drop the shirt off the back of Berry's shoulders, as Berry stepped out of her white jockey shorts. She stood naked for Vera's inspection for a moment, and then laid herself on top of the woman.

The satin of the corset was a revelation. Berry slid herself up and down over Vera's chest, mashing their tits together. She had a sense that Vera had stripped as far as she wanted to at this point, and moved in to take advantage of the tactile possibilities before her. She carressed Vera's uplifted breasts, running one hand down her side to her naked hip, playing with the elastic garter attachments, and stretching down towards the stockings. The transitions from satin to flesh to lace to silk were amazing, and she found herself repeating the movement, each time with greater pressure. She reached up behind Vera's neck to ruffle handfuls of hair, to scatter them around the pillow, around Vera's face, around her own arm.

For long minutes Vera took it passively, aware of Berry's pleasure in touching her, and then she brought her arms around the woman's back. She kneaded Berry's neck, shoulders, back, then hugged her close. They looked at each other, smiling widely, then

Berry laughed out loud. 'I almost forgot how it feels to be with someone incredible!' Vera didn't say anything, but she grabbed Berry and together they began to roll around on the bed, thighs thrust in between legs, arms grabbing and pressing.

'Should I take off your corset?' Berry asked.

'Can I leave it on? I'm kinda not into my tits hanging free ...' Vera answered hesitantly.

'Can you leave it on? Girl, you can do anything, anything, you wanna do. On or off, whatever, we're gonna have a good time.'

Berry rolled Vera onto her stomach and laid on top of her. Tossing her hair upwards, she managed to get a mouthful of the back of her neck, nipping and kissing and then biting a bit. She ground her pubic bone into Vera's ass crack and felt a responding pressure from the woman under her. She slid down lower, her fingers dragging down Vera's sides, and then pressed her tits into Vera's ass, which rotated in little circles on her chest. Getting on her knees between Vera's legs, she massaged her soft ass cheeks with her fingers, pulling them apart to open up her asshole, and then squishing them shut. She slipped her palms to the bottom of her ass and pushed upwards, as Vera arched her back automatically. Berry ran a finger from the top of the crack downwards, lightly tickling the woman's few hairs. Vera stopped arching her back; instead she pressed her pubes into the mattress as she felt a chill from each gently touched follicle.

Then Berry leaned over, drawing apart the cheeks and breathing into the crack. With her tongue she did the same gentle route that she had done with her finger, and again Vera pushed her ass out towards her. Just as her asshole seemed as open as it could be, Berry buried her face in the crack and began licking and probing with her tongue. She reached both hands around Vera's hips and her fingers made their way to Vera's clit. Sucking in the rear and strumming in the front, she felt that she had the whole world in her hands.

Meanwhile Vera was fighting off the disruptive thoughts which kept sneaking into her consciousness. 'Oh dear, I bet she'll see the stretch marks on my hips,' and 'I wish I could've showered when we got back here.' But once Berry's fingers began their wet massage of her clit, her id got the better of her superego. She just let go. The last thought she had was, 'Well, if she's already up my ass, I might as well enjoy it.'

And enjoy it she did. She could feel Berry's tongue inside her asshole, the one finger on her clit, and another running wetly along the passage between her cunt and her butt. But soon she became so aroused that there was no distinguishing between the different touches.

Berry did not stop until Vera, crying out, could take no more and lay limp and breathless across the bed. She sat up between the woman's legs, and noticed that her leather tie was lying entangled around Vera's wrist. In clutching at the pillow, Vera had, apparently, unknowingly picked up the tie. Berry unraveled it from her slack arm slowly, then crawled up to lie next to Vera, who immediately turned on her side to face the woman who had given her such delight. They hugged and kissed until Berry rolled her over on her back and sat up on her stomach. One hand pressing on Vera's chest for balance, she reached back with the other hand, and began dangling her tie in between Vera's legs. Puzzled by the sensation, Vera strained to raise her head so as to identify it.

'My tie,' Berry whispered, and Vera, with a quiet smile, let her head fall back. Running the tie between her legs, across her thighs, and then slapping it gently in her crotch seemed to reenergize Vera, who reached up to push Berry's shoulder, easily toppling her over next to her.

Now Vera sat on Berry's stomach, her garter extensions stretched out along her spread thighs, her nipples showing over the top of her firm satin corset. Berry had kept the tie between Vera's legs and with one hand held it from the back and with the other drew it from the front. Vera felt the stimulation, noted the muscles in Berry's arms where she strained to reach behind Vera to keep up the motion, but the focus of her concentration had changed. Leaning over, she let her hair fall onto Berry's face, and then with a brushing movement lightly whipped the woman's cheeks with thousands of delicate fibres. She changed the movement to up and down, running from Berry's face forward to her tits and back again. Berry lifted up her head for a moment and grasped a lock in her teeth, pulling Vera's head down to her. But Vera wasn't having any of it.

She freed her hair with her hands, then swiftly laid her whole length on top of Berry. Reaching to the floor on the side of the bed, she picked up her lycra leotard and slipped her hands into the arms of the garment. She began running her hands over Berry's body, scraping the slithery material roughly along the woman's skin. For the moment Berry forgot about the tie she was trying to control between Vera's legs, and sank back in surrender to the strange feeling. Vera's fingers stretched out the material tensely and she kneaded Berry's body, settling in on her tits which she pressed firmly with the palms of her hands, only to release into pinching fingertips. She slid her hands underneath Berry's tits and pushed upward strongly, squashing them like Berry had done to her ass cheeks.

Then she lowered herself between Berry's knee-bent open legs. She rubbed the woman's stomach, hips, thighs, calves powerfully, suddenly suspending all strength as she dangled the lycra material in Berry's crotch. At first she just tickled gently, then added little slaps with the loose arm-ends of the leotard. Finally she stretched it over her fingers again. With one hand she played with

Berry's clit and with the other she entered her cunt, the lycra-covered finger plunging in and out. Once it was soaked with Berry's wetness, she ran it up her crack and wiggled it at the entrance to her asshole, waiting to see what kind of response she would get.

Berry's responses were easy to read, because they were, you might say, loud and clear. She immediately moaned, breathing out an 'ahh-hh' and Vera knew that she was giving her new lover pleasure. She worked the wet material-covered finger into Berry's ass, feeling an initial resistance before it suddenly sank all the way in. With her middle finger she worked Berry's clit, then twisted her thumb into the dyke's cunt. Berry groaned and mumbled and reached her hands out towards Vera, who was too far away to touch.

'Put your arms down, relax,' Vera said softly, 'Just get into it.' Berry's arms hung in the air for a few seconds until the words seemed to sink in, and then she let them drop, one across her eyes and the other across her breasts.

Vera's fingertip made little circles inside Berry's ass tunnel, while her thumb alternately teased the cunt entrance and then thrust inward. But her other hand never stopped vibrating on Berry's clit. She carefully eased her finger out of Berry's ass, and when she noticed that the lycra leotard stayed inside, she began slowly stuffing more of it in. Once she had several fingerfuls up the dyke's ass, she removed her hands altogther, lowering her head to suck on her swollen clit. The rest of the leotard stayed bunched up in one hand, as she vibrated her tongue on the tip of the girl's clitoris.

Berry made more and more noise, but then fell silent. For what seemed like minutes, Vera could not even hear her breathing, until Berry gasped suddenly, taking in a huge toke of air; then once again held her breath. This happened twice, three, four times, until she began saying, 'Yes, yes, yes,' and Vera knew she was about to come. As Berry's body started trembling, she pulled the leotard straight out of the dyke's ass, and Berry nearly went wild.

After laying together quietly for some time, Berry wordlessly started unlacing Vera's corset. She opened a closet door next to the bed and pulled out a thick brown towel and a supersoft flannel robe, both of which she handed to Vera, pointing to the bathroom door. Vera smiled, got up holding her corset to herself, and when she turned to look before entering the bathroom, she saw Berry pulling back the bedspread to reveal black satin sheets. Berry looked up, Vera raised her eyebrows, and they both laughed with mutual satisfaction.

RESPONSE/ABILITY

ALISSA BLACKMAN

I

I never know how to ask her
how she likes fingers
tongue lips moustache hair
against wetness
goose bump skin
stiff leather
only fear she will no longer
have answers for me
leave me groping in the dark
and sucking in air like a blowfish
waiting for thin skin
waiting for the explosion.

II

My hands claw and rock
in her hair.
She smells like sweet shampoo
and dishwashing liquid.
My eyes are t-shirt blindfolded,
and my head presses
against the cool cool wall.
I am flowing top to bottom
my hands are kneading
her hair like bread
needing her hands
her mouth
her touch like bread.

SUDDENLY ONE SUMMER

ESTHER Y KHAN and L A LEVY

Staring at the instrument panel, Dalit's words seemed to fade into the distance, as my mind drifted back to the strange events of the last year.

Oy va voy. Six o'clock, the phone rings. I light a cigarette and turn up the answer phone volume.

'Oh yeah, screen your calls, turn your back on your friends.' It could only be Mina, her voice like iron filings.

For the past year we'd been thrown together, pursuing our crazy trail up garden paths and urban alleys. I took a break from everything I'd been doing; she took a year off from union fights, legal wrangles and political inroads. We decided to take action, no more words over restaurant tables, no more debate over beer and cigarettes, we decided to do it for real. Too many of our friends had been hit, too many questions hung in the air, something had turned our faded affair into a new partnership.

Our fees were way too low. Now I was independent, but lonely, a workaholic and living on peanuts. In this condition how could I find a lover? Since Mina ... no one. I was out of touch with the language of seduction. My once attractive slouch had got worse. I drank briefly, in bars, a little light chit chat, and home. That was my life, some life! Friends? They were going straight, or having babies, or getting seriously ill from over work. Bleak, and there's worse to come. Mina and me kept our just distance. We got close, and jumped apart, our relationship as lovers seemed to fall to pieces. Besides, the tragedy of it was swallowed up by daily professional hazards; stress, trauma, danger. I had no intention of picking up the phone.

I put on my reddest lipstick and walked luminously to the shops. Umyan, the Turkish Cypriot woman behind the counter worked a seven day week, and it showed. We exchanged our usual lame joke, and I left with some beer. Some days I consider myself fortunate.

Mina's message went like this:

'Dora Wolf left me a message, Lauren her cousin had a break-in. She says Lauren is completely crazy, but this seems serious. If you meet me outside Sandwich Scene in Wardour Street at eight thirty, I'll take you to her place. Leave a message if you can't make it.'

I drank some beer and listened to *'Hits of Colombia'* and thought it over for a while; then I went to meet Mina.

We fought our way through overflowing rubbish bags in a dark corridor that smelt like cat's piss. This was no palace, and when she finally answered her door, we found that Lauren Wolf was no princess. Her large eyes were surrounded by purple shadows, her cheekbones curved like urns, she had an intense, burning pallor. A biblical face, but crazy.

We sat in her bare room in front of a one bar fire, Lauren on a three-legged stool, Mina on a mattress, and me on the floorboards. Lauren went to the kitchen to fetch us glasses of water, and Mina and I exchanged a raised eyebrow. There was a length of wallpaper covered in frantic crayola spirals, and a mirror hung with chicken bones.

'Did you do those?' I asked.

Lauren glared at me.

'What I create scares people, I know. I'm not bourgeois, not classical enough for patriarchs and prissy feminists alike.'

Mina was staring at a collage of computer printouts, criss-crossed and shredded and hung with DHSS manilla envelopes and plastic bags of white powder. I changed the subject.

'So, what happened?'

'You mean the fascists?'

'You tell me.'

'Fascists, they smashed my door.'

'Why you?' Mina asked.

'They are mind terrorists, and they want to control me.'

'Did anything particular lead up to this?' I ventured, tentatively.

Lauren threw me a characteristic glare.

'Oh I see, Tracy the Dick, the little heroine is going to take on the forces of evil, huh? Well, Miss Amateur Dyke-Dick, check it out for yourself, I won't titilate you with details.'

'You should go and stay somewhere else for a while,' Mina cut in.

'Yes my dear, the streets and the hospitals, my homes from home,' Lauren choked on a laugh as she showed us the door.

Mina and I followed our glorious exit with an argument in the car. We ran around the streets bickering for a while, we lost each other, and Mina found me sulking in Brewer Street and offered to drive me home. We decided to work from separate corners for this one.

I'd woken early and gone straight over. A typical Soho morning. I had the whole day to work out the area. I started on Lauren's block, going door to door, posing as a market researcher.

Red lipstick, a layer of yellowish foundation, and giant earrings and I really looked the part. It's incredibly easy to get into people's homes. An actressy blonde, wearing pink rubber gloves and a floral wool dressing gown was prepared to tell me her life story, but didn't have much on Lauren.

A tousled teenager crawled out of bed to answer my knock. He stood framed in his doorway, and I could see a mountain of unwashed dishes and boarded up windows, as well as music and drug accoutrements. He invited me in for tea, but I declined, so he told me what he knew out in the hall. Lauren, or Karen, as he called her, wouldn't be interested in collaborating, he told me.

'You sure you're not a DHSS snooper?' he asked.

I tried not to look too shocked, and went upstairs. Everyone else was out, or not answering. These are days of long working hours.

I crossed the road and went into Sandwich Scene. I needed food. I could sit behind the plate glass and watch the world go by, and there was a perfect view of Lauren's block, and two or three buildings either side. I went up to the counter and ordered falafel and coffee. As I sat gazing out of the window, a plate of chillis arrived, balanced on a slim golden arm. I followed the arm to a denim-wrapped hip and up to her irises, polished mahogany, set like stones in the cool whites of her eyes. Her sleeve seemed to brush my cheek as she placed a knife and fork beside my plate. I watched her walking to and from the counter with a lilting, easy stride. I recovered enough to turn my attention to the dull red brick buildings in front of me, and began to eat the falafel, but her accent cut through my thoughts with a flash of recognition.

'It's okay?'

I jumped and mumbled some kind of affirmative.

I couldn't resist going back for a lemon tea later that day. The lunchtime rush was over and she sat next to me.

'Where are you from?'

I gave some kind of rendition of my jumbled origins, and she told me her father was also a Hungarian, and a refugee.

'Except yours ended up in Israel, and mine only got as far as London.'

'You want to come back at closing time?' she asked me, looking straight into my eyes.

I agreed without hesitation. That's how I met Dalit.

I went back to Lauren's in the meantime, and miraculously she was in, I felt lucky.

'So, it's Sherlock Shylock minus Dr Sidekick.'

I kept a frozen smile on my face and followed her into the kitchen. She was stir-frying on one ring. She offered me some limp carrots and beansprouts; the laws of hospitality are compelling, so I accepted.

'Well, Miss Market Research, getting friendly with the neighbours, huh?'

'I'm learning the trade,' I responded.

We crunched in silence for a while. My technique worked, Lauren spoke before I had to ask another awkward question.

'The organisation ... their roots reach wide and deep, they have many little shoots to do their work.'

'So who are we looking for Lauren?'

'Who are you looking for, count me out ...'

'So tell me something new.'

'Use your pretty little eyes, it's a big world out there, look for the real tough cookies and see how you stand up to the boot boys. I never laid a finger and look what they did to me. Leave them alone, ignore them, that's all I have to say.'

I told Lauren I'd be back and left. Out in the wide world I decided to follow my instincts. I tentatively trailed a couple of skinheads for a while and they led me to a leather shop in Carnaby Street. I figured I should be looking for the less obvious, but I didn't have a clue where to begin. It was getting on for five, nearly closing time at Sandwich Scene.

Delicious Dalit was up to her ears in salt beef, and changing tens to fives in the final rush. Sweaty guys in suits were finishing their meals, and Dalit cashed up and took off her apron. She emerged from behind the counter and grabbed my arm.

'Let's go,' she said. I floated behind her, out into the evening.

'What should we do?' Dalit asked.

'A club?'

'Too tired.'

'Dinner?'

'No more food please.'

'A film?'

'I couldn't concentrate.'

'My car's parked near by, we could go for a drive.'

As we walked it began to rain, cutting through the humid summer evening. The car took quite a while to start; Dalit put her hand on my thigh.

'Where shall we go?'

'Your place,' she said.

We stopped at the Casablanca super market and bought

everything you need for a romantic soirée, and with the radio on and Dalit's fingers laced through mine on the gearstick, we drove.

We kissed deeply and desparately in my doorway, as we climbed the stairs she held my waist and her mouth brushed my neck. We went straight to the bed, almost tearing off our shirts and lay breast to breast. I pulled away.

'I'm nervous,' I told her.

'Let's have a drink,' she said.

We took wine and glasses up on to my dangerously sloping roof, and I rolled a spliff. We talked, bits of our past, pieces of our dreams, skipping from one thing to another.

Our nervous panic over, we went to the bed, and taking our time, we got drunk on each other's touch. Her breasts were cool and fresh, her fingers hot and exciting. We fucked wildly, and gently, and hallucinogenically, we fucked with eyes wide open, and with eyes closed. The cars and the birds and grey dawn light cut into our sleep and we fucked again.

I made some coffee and we drank it in the bath. I poured water from her shoulders, watching it cascade down her chrysanthemum breasts. We sang to each other, underwater, imitating balalaikas.

We spent an hour dressing each other up, in dresses and stockings, suits and shirts, hats and jewellery.

'I have to go to work,' she said.

'Me too,' I replied.

I told her about Lauren and the fascists. She looked perplexed. 'You're crazy,' she said. 'Try living in Israel, London is easy, they're just little boys, dangerous little boys, leave them alone.'

'I can't.'

'Now that you have no enemy, you invent one, you give them power.' She gave me her jacket and took mine.

'Do me a favour,' I said. 'Just listen out at work, just keep a look out.'

'What should I look for, crazy punks with swastika tattoos?'

'Just look for the regular guys,' I told her.

She buttoned my jacket in a patronizing way, kissed my cheek and left. I found a note in her jacket pocket. It went:

'Your eyes are my oasis,
your hands are my heart
anything is possible ...
so meet me after work.'

... Or maybe I was just a one night stand? I spent the morning on the phone and in a big library full of homeless men with liquor in brown paper bags. I checked all the information on the links between fascist groups. A guy at an anti-fascist publication told me where all the organization bases were — all West End. These bastards were moving into the big time. He also agreed to send me some photos of known activists.

The phone rang, Dalit's gorgeous voice.

'You should know your friend is out on the street screaming at men.'

'And ...?'

'And that's it ... what else?'

'I'll call you back later.'

'Better late than never,' she spat, and hung up.

By the time I got to Lauren's nothing was happening, and she wasn't home. The neighbours eyed me with suspicion and said nothing. I called at Mina's and got her answering machine. I wondered if Mina had got there first. I was a bundle of tension when I got to Sandwich Scene, which was closed. A note was pinned to the door frame.

'I'm not a one night fling, get your ass down to Bar Deux, I'm there till eight.'

She was there, wearing shades in the corner. She handed me an envelope,

'A little gift for your detective persona.'

I pulled out a bundle of polaroids. Men's faces, real tough cookies, Lauren's worst nightmare.

'I should go to Lauren's.'

'On our date?'

'I'll be back in five minutes.'

'Okay, occupational hazards I guess, like me always smelling of falafel.'

'Five minutes,' I said.

I raced round the corner and along the street to Lauren's. No lights, no reply. I went back to the Bar Deux. Dalit was gone, but she'd left me a note. *'I'm tired, romance and fascism don't mix, call me.'*

I drove home, feeling upset and vaguely nauseous. Mina had called and the photos had arrived, hand delivered from the anti-fascist guy. At least some people took all this seriously. The photos matched the faces from Dalit's polaroids, and he'd attached a note. Lauren's father had been a 'nazi hunter', he had been active in Poland and after the war, he'd been working in Britain.

He'd died last year from a heart attack, and his work was unfinished. Lauren had cracked up after his death. Why hadn't Lauren told me this? I tried calling Mina again. Her answering machine clicked on, and gave out it's usual deadpan message.

I decided to go back over to Lauren's; I was worried and scared. As I approached her building I thought I could hear shouting. When I got closer I could see Lauren screaming through a letterbox. Three guys came out, heavy built, somehow familiar. I panicked; this was all happening too fast. I'd expected days of following empty leads and now ....

I quickened my pace and tried to think. Suddenly I felt someone behind me, and a second later a hand covered my mouth. I was hauled backwards, I could still hear Lauren. We were in her flat now, four men faced us pulling on gloves and assembling truncheons. These men are experts at fear and panic. Lauren was laughing and screaming:

'See what you get for your cynicism! No one believes and look, the forces of evil are real.'

I didn't have time to correct her assumption. The four men remained terrifyingly silent. I even prayed. While I waited in suspense for something to happen there was a crash. I couldn't make out what was happening, I was soaked in sweat and totally numb.

Mina and Dalit stood framed in the doorway, Cagney and Lacey style. Dalit held a gun, pointing it coolly at the heaviest of the men. The bastards were terrified. Dalit noticed their mood and fired at the wall for extra effect. The creeps fell to their knees. Looking extremely tough, standing behind Mina and Dalit, were Rafi and Asher, the cooks from Sandwich Scene. Dalit fired a few more shots at the wall, and sure enough the cops burst in, guns drawn, closely followed by the neighbour in the dressing gown, looking more ashen than actressy by now.

Mina, who could turn her hand to anything, gave a brilliant performance, explaining how we'd been having a little party when these guys broke in, and how we'd had to wrestle the gun off them. They roughed the creeps up, and bundled them off. A plainclothes detective stayed to take details, and our stories hung together. Mina and I did most of the talking. We went to the station to give statements, and even though they gave Rafi and Asher a hard time, it seemed beyond their imagination to think our story was a set up. Lauren had had the foresight to get a solicitor down there, so we were back on the street in no time.

The improbable story went like this ... Dalit and Mina had passed by Lauren's at the same time, and Lauren had come running out, screaming. The guys followed and bundled her back in the building. Dalit had run to a nearby bar to fetch Rafi and Asher, and back to the cafe to get the gun they kept behind the counter. Mina had gone to call me, and come back to find Dalit, Rafi, and Asher, on the verge of making their entrance. While they were gone, I'd arrived, like a comedy, without the humour. Lauren and I were almost casualties, but Dalit's stint in the army had finally proved useful. I asked Lauren why she hadn't told me about her father.

'Do I have to always be a victim of my history?' she'd answered.

Meanwhile Mina was eyeing Dalit with suspicion.

'Do you know each other?' she asked.

'It was a one night stand,' Dalit replied.

'Shall we go out and eat,' Mina suggested with astounding diplomacy.

Lauren's living with Mina now, and Mina's in local politics. The creeps got a few years for attempted murder. Dalit and me are lovers. Things are up and down ... but that's life. Nothing surprises me since that night, except Dalit.

◆ ◆ ◆

We'd been sitting in the car park of a Stamford Hill furniture store, reflecting on how that summer had changed our lives. We often went there on days off, to sit on the three piece suites, drinking the free coffee, and occasionally buying something in the sale. Although we lived separately, we'd become very home-oriented over the past year. Our flats were little palaces where we would escape from the stresses and the tensions of our working lives. Inside the showroom we found a corner with a bedroom set-up and sat on the edge of a giant mattress. The showroom was virtually empty, and the few assistants were assembled in a far corner chatting and drinking coffee. Dalit looked at me steadily, and slid one hand down the front of her jeans, which she wore several sizes too large, and with the other hand she undid her belt. She kept her eyes fixed on mine, smiling slightly. She began to move her hand round, in wide easy circles under her jeans. I leaned over to undo her zip, but she pushed my hand back to my own cunt. In the building excitement, I wrestled with my own button-fly, and moved my hand into a good position. I looked nervously around, but no one seemed to notice us. Keeping our eyes locked together we wanked slowly.

Dalit's face was deliciously flushed, and her eyes were becoming heavy-lidded. She slid her other hand into her open zip and I could see her fucking herself under the denim, I was getting very wet and I followed. I moved into a kneeling position and pushed two fingers into my cunt. The mattress was perfectly sprung, and we rocked gently until Dalit came, and then she put one hand on my ass until I came too.

I looked around and saw the assistants coming towards us, looking urgent. Dalit grabbed my hand and we ran across the showroom, down the stairs and out to the car park.

'That's the last time we can go there, I suppose,' Dalit laughed.

'Oh well, we'll have to find somewhere else,' I said, as we pulled into the stream of North London traffic, and away.

CANCER OF THE STARS

ELEANOR DARE

Wild nights. Diver couldn't help it. What else would rear its head in these parlous times but debauchery?

It was that sort of winter. People got cold at night — they welcomed her invitation to a fevered bed. The world had cancer. Everybody knew that. Fidelity seemed an unnecessary meanness.

Wild nights, while the planet warmed. Fucking in the very ocean track of hopelessness. The bitter waters piling up all around her.

Melting ice blocks at both poles had paradoxically sent shivers down the countries beneath them. Some places got hotter, others disappeared under ever swelling tides. But Diver's country cooled right down. And Diver needed other women to warm her. Without them she might flounder and the waters suddenly overwhelm her, filling her lungs below sea level.

When the water level rose everybody got scared, and the scarier things got the more Diver felt the desire to be cradled and succoured by welcoming lovers. And she in turn felt the impulse to give comfort. Sex was urgent. In the war against flooding, day to day sexual morals peeled away like the insubstantialities they had always been.

The governnment had predicted a certain loosening of conduct, and, hoping to prevent increased sexual activity, separated the sexes for their National Flood Training. During the six months residential course Diver attended, the women in her brigade had fucked each other like rabbits. As if fucking could suck up the flood tide. The ebb and fuck held in their mouths. And outstretched arms could cleave the anger of the sea.

Back in the city, when she wasn't working on the massive new flood barriers, Diver picked up dykes like there was no tomorrow. One evening at a public dining room Diver had sat down opposite a short woman with cropped black hair, all peppered over with flecks of grey like seal fur. She was about fifteen years older than Diver — getting on for forty, and she wore the uniform box pleat skirt of a flood coordinator. She looked like a sister swimmer to Diver — tight weather lines around her eyes, strong forearms. All through their drab government meal she watched Diver intensely. Then Diver felt a stockinged foot glide up between her legs and a very shipshape toe stroke the crossroad seam of her overalls.

They left together soon afterwards, pushing their way through a snaking queue of hungry flood workers.

'I'm not really this promisc ...'

'It's all right,' said Diver, taking the other woman's hand. 'The old rules don't count anymore.'

Despite the tentative tone of her first remark, the other woman calmly unbuttoned her own blouse as soon as they entered her flat, at the same time guiding Diver to her bed. Within seconds Diver had rolled down regulation stockings and placed her hands round the older woman's thighs, her mouth exploring smooth full breasts.

It had been a very swift introduction; soon Diver had done as her name suggested, plunging under the blue skirt, diving deep into the woman's velvet, nurturing cunt. She moaned for Diver to engulf her clitoris, holding the younger woman's head and directing it around her cunt. So fluid, Diver could gorge herself — sucking the other woman until she burst into orgasm. Returning the waters to their rightful place.

Outside the wind howled, it always did these days, sweeping across the city like the wind that swept over the emptiness before the Earth was made.

Diver had climbed onto the woman's impossibly soft belly, sliding her cunt against it, while the woman twisted and undulated beneath her. Diver riding a dolphin. Unwanted images of a still-dying, still-born planet only left her at moments like these. The other woman rocked her to orgasm. Only then, when their appetites were glutted, did they ask each other's names.

That winter was very long, and the news always got bleaker. It seemed to Diver that the whole world was suppurating. Even the stars showed signs of fatigue, languishing at night.

She worked on all the projects that were meant to 'save the people' — barriers and floating towns, but somehow they didn't reassure her. Everybody worked long shifts, but no one could out build the sea.

Sex was Diver's only stronghold. Fucking like death was on her shoulder. She knew it was neurotic behaviour, but she didn't give a damn. And besides — there were plenty of other women who wanted to make love as urgently as she did.

Two weeks after the dining room encounter, Diver met a woman she used to know before things had got so bad. They'd been very polite to each other in those days. None of this sexdesperation. They had wanted to sleep with each other but didn't because Floren was already in a relationship, and things like that used to matter.

Now the woman had been placed in her work team, and life moved on at a different pace.

About four days into their reunion, Diver had gone home with Floren to share a meal, one of those pretend spreads —

powdered eggs and soya loaves. Floren had popped out to fetch some ersatz ingredient for their supper while Diver fell asleep on a long comfortable couch.

She woke up when she felt Floren sitting beside the couch looking down at her, serious and washed out with a pallor of grief, which filled Diver with sorrowful lust. She reached up for Floren, gently pulling the other woman toward her, brushing the hair from Floren's eyes, then just holding her close until their mouths met and Diver's submariner tongue was warm against Floren's, their breathing accelerated, hands inevitably searching, pulling clothes aside. Diver feeling Floren's hand lightly pass across her vulva then return, sliding fingers into her open cunt, easy from Diver's wetness. Thrusting against Floren's hand, rocking with it, confused, thinking she was entering Floren. The two women holding onto each other, Diver arching her back so that their two wet cunts were moored together — coming together, creating their own flood.

Later that night they had gone to a government cinema, green river mist outside filling their mouths. Private individuals no longer owned televisions, they were a waste of valuable resources and a misuse of time. The large hall was packed, an old aerobics centre, complete with squeaky floor. People watched the flickering screen in silence as the news unfolded. Shit-loosening, disconsolate.

In Alaska all the children had died, bald headed and hallucinating. There was no explanation, it was simply presented as an act of God. But Diver suspected the ozone window above that country had opened to a lethal extent. The news rolled on.

Bangladesh had been thrown into a state of total emergency as the flood waters encroached. Millions of its citizens converging upon the highest borders, only to be met by barricades and battalions of armed soldiers. Her country had sent one or two aircraft carriers to collect refugees, but it was a half-hearted gesture. A feeble effort.

After that people got more scared. There were more floods. They broke up shifts and gave form to Diver's life. When she wasn't working — diving into the cold sea beneath the barriers, welding new defences, she slept with Floren and her other lovers.

And that was how time passed — season after season. Until finally, all the barriers were finished. And then the tidal waves came.

Thrashing against all their fortifications, tearing them asunder, so that the Earth was without form and void, with darkness over the face of the abyss, and a mighty wind that swept over the surface of the waters.

IMPRECISE COMPLICATIONS

STORME WEBBER

or did you really mean/what you didn't say?
once again ...
chaka wd say 'why is it i'm always chasin after you ...'
well not exactly ...
but i feel a resistance when i'm wanting to hold you
next to me/ and plunge underneath the next wave
feel that delicious terror until we emerge
streaming water and gasping for breath.
is it that you don't want to risk the unknown?
i know we wd come out safe
on the other side.
so i suppose i'll keep on playing
in this ocean/ till i convince yr
faith in the grace of yemanya
we can go as far into this pure feeling
as we want/ she won't let us drown.
ecstasy is no mystery
if you believe.

TAKE YOUR CLOTHES OFF

JEANNIE BREHAUT

I've been back in London since yesterday. Before that I was in the Canadian Rockies. A whole year of working for Jane and living with Jane until one day I woke up towered over by God's best mountains, and it was ordinary. At night after that, Jane and I, you know — we started to only sleep. It's not that I have to have sex every night or anything but I've got to feel cherished. I started to hate the mountains. I hated the quiet and no real sunsets and how everybody, especially Jane, only thought about their mountain bikes and making more money. She'd work three jobs in one day and then roll away from me like a dead person. I would lie there thinking, 'Okay Andrea, what are you going to do? You're obviously not happy anymore.'

I had enough money in my bank account for a one-way ticket here. I phoned Judy and told her to meet me. She said she would and wasn't it funny because she had just seen you that morning. I felt like a kid all the way flying out of Canada, Morgan, too excited to read a word, thinking about you and my heart jumping. Do you know that at twenty-five I've become what I always wanted to be — a world traveller. I have come a bigger circle than the whole globe, moving from loving no one to loving you, to the others, and then Jane and now you again — my darling. I may be romantic but I'm still tough. Look for me in leather.

Judy met me at the airport and gave me your address and then I put my bags in storage. I have a bit of money and I can stay with Judy but I must admit I plan to live with you from now on. I walked clean out of the airport and onto a bus. Later I will tell you about Jane and you can tell me what I've missed in London. I just want to walk with my arms around you along the South Bank where I hear there are now a million gay girls. People looking at you like they always do because you are so lovely. I'm going to feel the way I discovered when I met you, tipped forward and something in my knees so that every step I take is wonderful. In the beginning, when we used to take turns and just talk and touch each other, do you remember how it was with us?

You lived in a different place now, Morgan, but were you the same? I didn't have time to think about it. The bus let me off on the corner of Clapham Common and I bought you flowers from a man in a shop who I swear wouldn't stop smiling. Then I ran all the way along the south side to your house. Champagne, your wonderful cat, was stretched out in the windowsill and I wanted to cry at that moment. Streetlamps up and down the south side blazing for me and Champagne with her green eyes full of wonder. Have you ever seen a cat glad to see a person? I've never come home like this before. I loved everybody. I just stood there and had that feeling. Andrea Elizabeth Cunningham — this is your life.

Then I knocked.

Champagne sprang off the sill and I heard you coming down the hall. Morgan, I wanted to hug you and kiss you and undress you in full sight of everyone. But you looked at me and I knew I wasn't welcome. There was the coldest chill when you opened that door. I felt it but then your hall was warm and you were inviting me into your flat without looking at my eyes and introducing me to some kid named Lucy. Who the fuck was Lucy? Champagne just stared at me, like don't ask. I cuddled Champagne and I was in shock. I just couldn't help it. I kept kissing Champagne's paws and saying, 'Well, at least somebody is glad to see me around here.' I was ashamed of it later but that's the way it happened. I wanted you alone so I could talk to you and explain why I left Banff and show you my beautiful mountain body. There was something wrong with you, I could tell. You kept buzzing around, picking things up, wiping them off. Lucy was staring at me, she was really interested. There is no way to explain the rest of the night, no matter how I tell it. I had come three thousand miles to take you in my arms, Morgan. I couldn't go away alone after that.

Lucy and I went to the clubs that night. You washed all your dirty dishes and tidied up a kitchen full of plants. I got one word answers and your back for half an hour. I didn't remember you having so much hassle around you before.

You didn't seem to mind when we left together. It was too weird — Lucy and I standing outside Clapham Common station talking sweetly to each other. I said,

'So what's the story? Are you and Morgan ...?'

She just kept looking at me with a really golden expression.

'Andrea, we are sometimes. But I'm not thinking about her right now.'

You'll never believe this but I wanted that girl then, standing under a streetlamp outside the tube station. Wanted her in a different way than how I still wanted you. You are right, she is beautiful. You can have passion for more than one person if you like.

We got onto one of those crazy Friday night trains going up the Northern Line toward everybody's favourite party. Crowded in a car with all these drag queens, we kept smiling at each other. She's only a kid, eighteen years old last weekend. I guess you knew that. I guess you two celebrated her birthday together. I'm sorry Morgan. I've been away from all this too long. I used to handle love on the rocks a lot better. D'you remember when we first met each other? I'll never forget that night.

Lucy and I changed trains and got out at Green Park.

'We can walk from here,' she said.

'Okay.'

She was leading. She was leading and I was glad to be back in London. Clubs move around all the time, I didn't know the one we were going to. We went towards Pall Mall and then back on ourselves in the direction of the park.

'It's too early to go to a club.' Lucy looked at me in the dark. 'Come with me.'

'Where? The park will be locked.'

'Just come with me. Through here. Don't worry.'

The traffic noises were fading. Lucy took my hand. I could smell that earth smell London has this time of year, sort of shitty and wonderful. There was no arguing with her. We went in behind some trees and through a break in the fence.

'I don't know if this is safe.'

She took me toward the centre of the park.

'Here.' It was a mound of earth, protected on all four sides by bushes and then trees.

'We're not supposed to be in here.'

'Shhh,' Lucy said, 'just listen.'

There was no sound, nobody near. She took off her jacket and put it on the ground.

'Lie down.'

'Not here?' She must be crazy. I was laughing a little.

'Please.' Her voice was sweet, teasing. 'It'll be okay, just do it.'

I was going to make a joke about whether or not she did this with all the girls and then I saw her face.

The best ride in this whole world is being wanted that much. It was the same hot look I saw on her face in the kitchen. Lucy knew she and I could be in a thing together. Even if she does live with you, Morgan. I lay down because I like her and I couldn't hear anybody nearby. Besides I'm tired of bedrooms and knowing what's going to happen. In the dark I could see treetops and feel the ground under me, cold and breathing. Then there was nothing in front of me except her face.

We kissed. We kissed and she was on me. Pouring her eyes into me, her tongue burrowing. Holding me down like an expert. Eighteen, jesus. If later ever came I was going to have this girl's entire history. Where, and from who, did she learn how to dance?

Our shirts were open. She bit my nipple and then pulled. I was moaning. I wanted her gorgeous tits in my mouth that minute. There was a bit of a struggle for who sucked who, but she was holding me, remember. I relaxed because what were my choices? Then what started happening became forever. I went somewhere with her I've never been before; gave up.

'Take your clothes off.'

I sat up to do it and she supported me. All at once Lucy was squeezing my skin, holding the small of my back in one hand, pushing me forward. I lay on the earth, stomach down, and she stroked me gently. I was wet and ready. She felt me and then plunged into my vagina. Her whole arm in me, maybe. Lucy leaning out across my buttocks — her hand up inside me, rocking. I was a beautiful thing on the earth and I was burning. She moved the way she had to and I followed. Rocked me and then raised me up, both of us panting. All the people I call for when the unbelievable is happening.

'Jesus. God, help me.'

'Turn around, on my hand, slowly. I want to see your face.'

She has to have me like this. I look at her and she is kissing me, pulls her hand out, then plunges deeper. She loves every minute of this, every inch of me. Then, Oh God, she is kissing me there and my hands dying in her hair and I am coming all over her face.

I remembered where we both were and for a minute I was frightened.

She says, 'I have something in my bag for you.'

A dildo. She carries a dildo. Who is this girl anyway?

'This will be so fucking incredible with you.' She's excited and happy. 'Lie down. That's right.'

'Keep kissing me and don't stop.'

I can feel her hands between us. She holds one end of the dildo against her pelvis, finds me and then both her hands grip my shoulders. She slides the dildo into me and rocks her pelvis gently. I say her name over and over, watch her face. All of her over me and inside of me and for her, the pride of doing. I open my legs wider, rise up to meet her. She needs me and it feels so good, what she's doing. I grab her soft bum and pull her down bringing the dildo she has deep into me. She shudders and for that moment her face is the most beautiful. Tells me how she wants me to move and I do it. I take the whole dildo and she is pressed right up against me, rocking and moaning. Under my hands her skin is soft wet, the girl smell of her exploding. She rolls me on top of her and we go further. I open for her and ride her, take her into me. I move for her and tell her how I love what she's doing. I arch for her and she fucks me deeper than anybody. She is all mouth, girl's arms, the concentration, her young tensed body. Rushes me again and again and I'm so glad, all her beautiful pushing.

Lucy sits up.

'Do you care if Morgan finds out we're here together?'

'Yeah. Yes, but not more than what you're doing.'

Lucy looks at me only. 'I won't stop.'

Lucy doesn't need to stop. Morgan won't know. All the way home from Canada I leaned into Morgan with my hottest dreams and she didn't feel me. There was that awful look she gave me when she opened her front door but I can't remember the feeling now. Lucy kisses me and from here there isn't another woman waiting for me anywhere. Lucy kisses me again and I have no past.

EAT

SAPPHIRE

'You too good to eat my pussy?' she snorted.

I don't believe she said that.

Sunlight strained through deep purple velvet curtains, breaking through the white lace which was draped in front of the velvet. Fontaine sat at the head of her big comfortable bed surrounded by her dusty finery. Her body seemed like a series of alabaster poles resting blankly inside blue denim.

'Cough syrup?' she queried.

I nod.

'It's from China,' she informs me, 'high opium content.'

'Really,' I murmur, 'I thought they weren't into that anymore.'

'It's not from *that* China,' she spit out.

'Oh scuze me,' I said apologetically.

Bob Dylan poured aquamarine and indigo from the stereo ...

with your mercury mouth in the missionary times

'Did ya hear what I said?'

'Yeah, about China.'

'No,' she said emphatically,' 'bout eating my pussy.' Wow,

this was deep. I wanted the cough syrup but I wasn't going to fuck for it.

'Here.' She shoves me a dark amber bottle in a crumpled paper bag, I hand her a twenty. I look down at my string bag on the floor, filled with bread, cheese, and sweet gold-flecked green grapes. The sounds of the street seep in through the window. I had forgotten about Fontaine the six years I'd been away. I'd been walking from one end of the city to another the day after my aunt's funeral when my feet had stopped in front of the old hotel, remembering what I'd forgotten — the music: Jimi, Janis, Buddy Miles; water pipes, syringes, acid and strawberry wine and Fontaine. I couldn't imagine she still lived there. I couldn't imagine her living anywhere else though, I'd thought, as my feet padded across the faded maroon carpet, my nose taking in the odour of old wood, perspiration and cigarette smoke.

'Miss Fontaine please, room 522,' I had asked the faded little man behind the desk.

'Go right up,' his voice limped softly.

It seemed like years now since I had stepped out of the elevator and through Fontaine's door. I glanced at my watch, it hadn't been years, I'd only been sitting there for fifteen minutes or so. Fontaine gaunt and emaciated stared at me with hard eyes. Anorexia, I thought, reaching for my bag.

'You just got here!' she wailed.

Dylan crooned:

with your sheets like metal and your belt like lace
and your deck of cards missing the jack and the ace

She was dying and I was leaving as fast as I could get up and get out of there. But I didn't go. I sat there staring at her quilt, astrological symbols on yellow squares. I looked at her shiny black leather riding boots. She looked at me looking.

'Brand new,' she shrugged gesturing to the boots. 'Never wore 'em before.'

My knees felt like they had rusted but somehow I got up. I moved away from the curtains fighting the light, away from the red roses on the yellow squares. The door was not far, I would get there.

sad eyed lady of the lowlands
where the sad eyed prophet said no man comes

I look back at Neptune on blue velvet and her long white arms coming out of her denim jacket.

my warehouse has my Arabian dreams should I put them
by your gate

Against the deep purple drapes she is whiter than the white lace.

oh sad eyed lady should I wait

Bones are revealed in stark relief as she strips away her clothes. Her body is an elongated tear. I am standing where I had been sitting. My feet move but not where I told them. I am kneeling besides her now, helping her slide the hard boots off her feet, one, then the other. Now the jeans, I gasp at the cavern between the two pale flares of her pubic bones. I pull her pants off dropping them besides the bed. Her arm goes around my neck like a hook.

'Wait,' I plead. Her smell is harsh — fear, nicotine, perfume. No heat, no sex-odour.

My breasts drop from my bra, warm with the heat of my body. Opening my jeans I am aware of the roundness of my brown belly as I slide my pants down. Dropping my pants on the floor next to hers I pull back the quilt, pull up the wrinkled sheet and slide under the covers like a little girl. My hand on her arm tells her to do the same. Her eyes are silent beggars. I pull her on top of me. She seeps into me like sand. My hands move slowly over the psychic battlefield that is her body, over the war she is losing. Sadness fills me. My hand spans her thigh, her buttocks. Hold her, *hold her*, hold her my soul screams. And it feels good so good to hold someone. I stop being horrified at what she has lost and marvel at what she has — life, breath, her legs between my opening thighs.

'Turn over,' I whisper. Prayerfully my hands begin to move over her body like the wind, everywhere, finding armpit, shoulder, neck, lips, thighs, knees, breasts, stomach, buttocks, eyebrows, hair. I am putting a shell to my ear, trying to hear the sea. She begins to talk like the sea does, in whispers, moans, churnings. I move down in the bed and pull her vagina to my mouth. My tongue searching for life between her legs. One orifice pressed to another, to suck. First thing we know to do when we born, suck — or die. My tongue beats her clitoris, joy spreading over my face as the sea begins to flow in my mouth.

'Please,' she whispers.

I keep on, my mouth a warrior in a pink battlefield pushing back death. Feel, feel, *feel*, I will. Her body begins to rock in the old time rhythm and I know it won't be long. I keep on and on, her body mine, mine hers. I feel the soft moans coming from her throat before I hear them. My will is transformed to power. I pull her on top of me and we press our bodies together rocking like Naomi and Ruth musta rocked. She pulls my head back down between her legs, the taste is alive in my mouth. She comes again and again. We hold each other quiet, long. She laughs like a warm soft bird in my arms. Stroking my face she whispers,

'Momi, what can I do for you?'

I hesitate for a second, then reach for the string bag on the floor, pull out the sweet grapes, holding them to her mouth I say,

'Eat.'

DOLPHINS

CAROLINE HALLIDAY

as slippery as dolphins you surprised me
with that diving under & below
biting and juicy with it
flesh that leapt
leaping from your mouth
to rest and leap and rest some more

I lost the measure of which
part of me swept feeling
through and through, which part
was mouth plunged, tongue,
and which rose, tricky and certain,
eager to tease, and play

no need for surfeit, no need,
time plentied on my body
time waited like a black fish,
silver with pleasure,
slippery for thumb and hand and
tongue, meeting again and over,
& again meeting, till
rich and silver vortexed, slid
into the moon into the
silver black night of our
bodies and beyond

MAEVE AND BETH GO SHOPPING

CHERRY SMYTH

'It all began with Auntie Vi,' Maeve said suddenly.

A short, sleepy groan emerged from the crumpled duvet.

'Well, she was my great aunt, actually.' Maeve went on. 'Every afternoon, after lunch, Auntie Vi and Auntie Florrie would go for a lie-down. I'd sit on the eiderdown and watch them undress, letting their huge, pale bosoms fall from stiff bras and wide hips spread, as they rolled down their twenty-four hour girdles. It was splendid. Then we'd all put on pink, fluffy bedjackets, smelling of Apple Blossom talc and get into bed.'

'Maeve, I'm asleep. It's Saturday morning. Keep your voice down.'

'But imagine, Beth, the feeling I had being nestled between them! It was safe in there and so sensual. They'd tell stories until they would go asleep, and I lay and watched their faces become soft and peaceful.'

'Yeah, like mine was a few moments ago. What time is it?' Beth asked.

'Half nine. Time to get up. We've got to go to Safeways.'

Maeve was resiliently bouncy. Beth gave in. She moved her braids out of her eyes and yawned.

'So what age were you anyway?'

'From nought to five or six. I stayed with them a lot before primary school started.'

'And what all began with Auntie Vi? Your love for big breasted women, or your need to blather when you're in bed?' Beth asked drily, stretching her legs down the warm sheets.

'No, my fantasy of being in bed with two women.'

'You should try it. You get everything you want from all sides, and more,' Beth said in her cool lover tones.

'I will, I will. Give me time,' Maeve replied with mock peevishness.

Beth laughed and leaned on her elbow to look at Maeve, who lay with her arms behind her head, red hair sticking up like a prep school boy's, her hazel eyes bright and awake.

'Anyway, I thought *that* fantasy began with your French teacher and the language assistant.'

'No, it started with Auntie Vi and was fuelled by what I saw in the school storeroom.'

'Tell me about it,' whispered Beth coaxingly. She moved to rest her head on Maeve's breast and run her fingers up and down her side. Maeve's skin flickered under the surface.

'Well,' she began, 'Mrs McAleese doesn't sound very sexy, or very French either, but she was beautiful — quite strict, but beautiful. She was from Brittany. She'd long black hair which she wore in a bun, *chignon*, and blue eyes. She dressed in smart trouser suits. She taught verbs by rote, and made us recite them at the front of the class. When she said, "Very, very good, Maeve", I would glow for the rest of the day. She was so hurt and disappointed when I didn't get it right I felt dreadful humiliation. I was almost nauseous.'

'What did she say?'

'She would shake her head and look away as if I'd said something cutting. I think that's when I most wanted to touch her and take her head in my hands and stroke her cheek. I wanted her to forgive me. I'd blush and stammer an apology and retreat to my desk, utterly ashamed. The fantasy was always strongest when she seemed to reject me. I wanted her to ask me to stay behind after class. She would order me to come up to her desk and beg forgiveness. I'd have to go down on my knees and cling to her trouser suit. Overwhelmed by my passionate dejection, she'd haul me up and hold me, caressing my hair. Then she'd slowly kiss my cheeks and murmer, "Petite cherie" and I would faint.' Maeve's voice fell from the excited crescendo with a sigh.

'You're such a drama queen, sweetheart. I was busy fucking my way through my dorm, while you were having *Maidens in Uniform* hot crushes. So chaste!' She moved her wide hips over Maeve's cunt and motioned back and forth. Morning lust travelled up and down her body.

'So what happened when the assistant arrived?' asked Beth, her voice low and flirtatious, her mouth teasing Maeve's ear.

'That's when it all hotted up, my love. Mademoiselle Laclos was with our class for a term to train as a French teacher. She was from Senegal. She was tall and slim with large breasts and the most beautiful straight, wide nose. She'd tight curly hair and a wild chuckle that seemed to put Mrs McAleese right off her stride. They were wary at first. I suppose they were in awe of each other's gracefulness. Then they began to whisper conspiratorily in rapid colloquialisms. Mrs McAleese's gestures expanded and loosened in response to Mademoiselle Laclos's animation and a knot of discomfort choked my solar plexus. It was like not being chosen at games.'

'The beast of jealousy writhed in you!' Beth said sardonically.

'Exactly. I felt sick and confused. I told no one.'

'Poor baby. Unrequited love at thirteen.' Beth wanted to move her hands down Maeve's thighs, to take a nipple in her watering mouth. 'Go on,' she said simply.

'Once I came into the classroom during lunch. It was empty. I heard laughter from the storeroom. I'd recognize that laughter anywhere. I imagined them touching each other, having the pleasure of feeling beneath their clothes, the anxiety of knowing that they could be caught at any moment. I wanted to scream and run out. Yet I stood entranced by the storeroom door. My urge to be included was stronger than my rage and hurt. I crept up to the keyhole and looked in. Mademoiselle was sitting on top of the small step ladder, her skirt pulled up around her thighs and Mrs McAleese was crouched down, her head between Mademoiselle's legs.'

'My god, man!' gasped Beth. She felt wet trickle out of her cunt. She needed to be touched. She took Maeve's hand and moved it between her thighs. Maeve continued talking, her voice breathless, persistent.

'Did you go in?' asked Beth, with excitement.

'Shhh and listen,' Maeve scolded. 'I couldn't move. I was terrified. My legs were completely weak. My hands sweaty. I needed to go to the toilet. My gym knickers were damp. My heart had just done the hundred metres hurdles.'

Maeve's fingers circled Beth's clit as she spoke and felt her labia swell and separate. Beth sucked one of Maeve's hard nipples and gently squeezed the other.

'Shall I stop the story?' asked Maeve sternly.

'No please, go on, please,' Beth pleaded.

'As I watched, Mademoiselle began to toss her head, her breath growing shorter. Then she started to shake and close her thighs around Mrs McAleese's head. Mademoiselle bit her fist and I heard a low moaning sound. Mrs McAleese lifted her face. It was radiant. Strands of her neatly tied up hair had fallen around her mouth. Her lips and chin glistened. She looked at Mademoiselle. They both smiled and fell into each other's arms. I yearned to open the door, be invited in. I wanted to be held, be touched, be taught. I wanted them to show me what to do that made them look so wordlessly wonderful. If only I could have buried my head in Mademoiselle's breasts and caressed her, while Mrs McAleese watched. Mademoiselle would undress me, cup my small breasts, seduce me slowly with Mrs McAleese's approval. Then ultimately, *she* would have me. She would lick me all over, bewilder me with passion and then allow me to touch her, make her wet for me, make her moan and scream with pleasure. She would be mine. My hand turned the door knob. Suddenly the bell rang breaking my desire, propelling me away from the door and out of the classroom where I stood in the corridor, pent-up and shaken.'

Beth sighed through clenched teeth, 'Go inside me. Fuck me!'

And Maeve held her as Beth's cunt drew in her fingers. Beth came, digging her hands into Maeve's shoulders, straining her neck back, until the veins rose beneath the skin.

'I'll teach you, babes.' Beth said slow and quiet, her dark eyes calm. 'Turn over.'

'But what about Safeways?' asked Maeve.

'To hell with Safeways. I'll treat you to a meal tonight and take-aways all week. Okay?'

'Hmmmm.' Maeve smiled and turned over.

AGROLOGY

TERRI L JEWELL

We met in Arkansas.
    You invited me to till your loam,
    sift for seasoned scents with delicate vision,
my tongue dipping litmus to gauge your tart hollows.
We smelled the grasses stripped of their seed
and chewed vanilla pods of the wild climbing orchid,
planted our fingers
    that emerged cress and pomegranate
    to fall and sprout again and again.
Earth began its rumble.
Tectonic plates slid and broke,
peaked into your shoulders, your breasts.
    The thick bows of our lips composed musics
    Ashanti, Kikuyu, Fulani, Ibo.
We met in Arkansas.
    Your buttocks rained a moister substance,
    soaked fertile rows down to bedrock.
Our roots enwrapped excuses, crushed them to powder,
drove the thirst ever deeper between us.
I feigned scientist for your cryptic equations
    as you lay decisively fallow,
    vows of rebirth hot in your eyes.

SHERLOCK HOLMES AND LA DOLCE VITA

ISABEL ROSS

'So I'll see you at the ABC, quarter past seven? Right, 'bye.'

I wait, deliberately, until her phone goes down at the other end, then put my own receiver back as carefully as I can. Lately, I have taken to banging doors, revving engines and slamming the phone into its cradle when I'm upset and I don't want either Rachel or Catherine, who is sitting at her desk beside me, to know just how childishly angry and disappointed I feel.

I could weep with frustration. I've been looking forward so much to seeing her this evening and I have made the usual mistake of planning how I would like it to be: garlic bread, a Greek salad with lots of basil, olive oil and onions, blackcurrant cheesecake, the MacGarrigle sisters on the stereo, followed by Leonard Cohen — 'There ain't no cure for love' — a bottle of fizzy white from the off-licence, flickering candles and fire and the two of us sunk in the soft folds of the downie in front of the sofa ....

And now it seems she wants to go to see a *film*. I grew up going to the pictures once a week with my Dad. I love films, truly I do. But I don't want to go to one tonight. I do not want to sit with her in a dingy, smoky atmosphere with lots of other people. I do not want to breathe in their Superkings, listen to them chomping their popcorn, smell their horrible perfume and the tomato sauce on their burgers. I want to be close to her in our own space where I can get high on the taste of her smell, look at her, where we can .... No, I won't think about it just now. My body will start heating up and sending off sex signals and Ted will assume, as men always do, that they are directed at him. This could lead to the third offer of a drink and a lift home. I suspect he feels sorry for me, and is kindly planning to offer me some much-needed male attention. *Poor Bel — forty-five if she's a day, no husband, why don't I just do her a favour? The wife needn't know ...*

At the moment, *I* feel sorry for myself, but not because of lack of man hours.

'What are you going to see?' asks Catherine.

'*La Dolce Vita,* the new version,' I say. How could Rachel do this? Is she just sending me up? She knows how I hate all that exploitative stuff, women distorted into the shape that men would have them be, conspicuous consumption, machinery and noise all against a background of nice, normal, heterosexuality ... *aargh!*

Rachel loves to tease me and I know I have to grow up and accept it. She thinks — quite rightly — that I am horribly insecure and over-sensitive. And perhaps she really wants to see the bloody film.

My love of films is mostly confined to Hollywood — my Dad's taste ran to Doris Day and John Wayne, my own to Yul Brynner (*s-t-r-a-n-g-e*), Barbara Stanwyck, Judy Garland. True, I did think Anna Magnani was fantastic in *Wild is the Wind,* but then that was her Hollywood phase. Nowadays I find that I'd like to see *Desert Hearts* and that French film with Miou-Miou at least once a fortnight and am longing for someone to film *Patience and Sarah,* but *La Dolce Vita*? The last time I saw an Italian film — *L'Avventura* — I nearly passed out from boredom.

Loving Rachel has revived the child in me. I want all my wants gratifed now. Most of my wants are centred on her — I want to be with her. I want to be beside her. I want to be in her. I want her all the time. And I don't want to share my time with her with other people. My Calvinist conscience tells me I shouldn't be like that. Rachel tells me I shouldn't be like that. So when she rings me up to say, do I mind if we go to a film instead of staying at home, I stifle my grief and rage and say no, of course not, that will be fine, where shall we meet? I cannot quite stifle the urge to ask if we can go back to my place afterwards. She laughs indulgently, yes. The MacCleay heart returns to a size which can be contained within its ribs — I'm not losing a whole evening of her.

I am totally confused by this desperate reliance on another person for my very happiness, for even a basic physical ease. Having fought my way out of a stifling marriage to some form of independent existence, I did not expect to be pole-axed by a small, vivid woman with a bizarre taste in clothes and a stronger and better-developed sense of independence than my own. I know that for my own sake and hers, I must hold on to a clear self-image, not let myself merge into her. Above all, I must not expect her to merge herself into me. But I wake up wanting her and she has taken up centre stage in my dreams and now I've got to waste an agonizing hour and a half watching androcentric celluloid before I can be alone with her.

I try to concentrate on work for the rest of the afternoon, stay on for an extra hour to try to leave my desk in a state which will not add to the problems of the morning after. I know I will be down tomorrow morning because it will be another thirty-six hours until I can see her again. Is this a common phenomenon — the way love makes time elastic — stretching to infinity when you're without *them* and concertina-ing when they're there?

At home, I change into clothes to compensate my skin for the prolonged absence of her — soft bra and pants, silk shirt and slip, floaty lawn skirt, high-heeled leather shoes. Technically, I should be cold, but I'm burning up with the thought of getting my hands on her after the film. I throw on my soft woollen coat, coil a long silk scarf round my neck and dash off to the cinema. At the last minute, I pick up the bag of fleshy tomatoes, olives, emerald peppers, creamy feta cheese, bread and wine which were to have been the start of a wonderfully erotic evening. There might at least be time for food ....

On the bus, I wonder what Rachel will be wearing. She is a designer of children's clothes and believes in self-expression. She has appeared as a garden gnome — yellow dungarees, cute little green boots; a very ambitious business woman — severe charcoal suit, tie, the lot; sensuous sybarite — flowing with velvets and silks and gauzy wool. I like that persona. Often she looks just plain strange and not, shall we say, her best.

I sometimes find myself feeling a bit nervous at being seen with her, but I soon get lost in her vivid recounting of her day, her excited exposition of some new idea, the heat of her eyes .... Stop it. I pull myself together. We are going to spend the next hour and a half in the company of up to three hundred people. We won't be able to talk. I won't be able to look at her. My heart is sinking again. I know I am going to sulk. I have to get this under control.

There she is. Good God, I know it's cold, but that's ridiculous. She is wearing a loden green cape, à la Sherlock Holmes, complete with cape shoulders, buttoned to the neck. Brown leather boots and long gloves. I'll have to wait until after Fellini's masterpiece to find out what has triggered off this particular bit of costume drama.

As we buy our tickets and go to our seats, I ask about her day and devour her face and hair with my eyes. My heart is swelling up again — or are my ribs getting tighter? I don't know which it is, but I know it happens everytime I see her. As always I look for signs of her disapproval of me, some clue to why she didn't want to spend the evening as we have done before, wrapped in each other's bodies. I learn nothing. She seems happy and pleased to see me.

I take off my coat and Rachel murmurs her approval of my bottle-green silk blouse, caresses my sleeve with the lightest touch of her fingers. I admire the gloves she has unbuttoned and is slowly peeling off. They are beautifully soft, smell slightly musty, but are warm from being on her hands. Rachel loves the idea of old clothes which have been cherished by their owners long ago. These she got at a jumble sale, of course. She has an unerring eye for a bargain.

The film begins and I remind myself that this couple of hours is not totally wasted. She is sitting beside me. I am actually with her. But ... I can't see her. I want to touch her; it isn't possible with all these people and all these clothes.

Rachel makes a couple of comments about the opening sequence. I turn slightly towards her so as to be able to answer without disturbing the others round us — and so that I can steal the occasional glance at her while she watches the film. The flickering light from the screen changes the planes of her face as I watch. She catches my eye, gives me a slightly stern look and fixes her eyes back on the picture. I feel the desire to sulk rising up in me again. Why can't we be at home? We'd be onto the cheesecake by now. Except I left it behind.

Feeling the slightest touch on the back of my hand, I look down to see her right hand lying in my lap, and quickly lace my fingers into hers. This is nice. My bottle-green sleeve, and the folds of her loden cape, hide our hands, her bare arm. The wool of her cape is surprisingly soft against the back of my hand. Cosy. I begin to feel better. Maybe the film isn't so boring after all.

I especially love her hands — slightly plump, white with lots of freckles, some now merging into age spots. Her grip on mine tightens. I glance at her, but she is still immersed in the film. She shifts her position, turning slightly towards me, and draws my hand through the arm-opening of her cape. My arm slides across satin lining, slithery over the folds of woollen cloth. She guides my hand on to warm smooth flesh. Bliss. Yes, this is definitely nice. I can tolerate all that *imbroglio* on the screen if I can sit in contact with her like this.

I stroke her skin. Heaven. I allow my mental picture of her to focus a little, seeing the tiny scar on her fourth rib. I move my fingers to find it. There it is, a crescent moon of taut, thin parchment. There is something strange, though. I feel lost in unfamiliar territory.

Am I inside her shirt? Dress? I climb a little and the back of my hand feels the weight and heat of a breast. The blood begins to pound in my head. I don't understand. My hand can move about at will. No buttons scrape my fingers, no seams restrict their freedom. Is she wearing some sort of loose silken smock? I turn a little further towards her, reach up between her breasts to find a collar. There is nothing. She isn't wearing a shirt, anything. Trembling, my hand cups down over each breast in turn. Rachel gives me one glittering glance, then continues, apparently, to concentrate on the screen.

Her nipples are erect, hard as dates, the aureoles knobbly as walnut shells, but hot, hot and dry. I cannot believe this. My outer self is sitting politely in a cinema looking at a 30 × 30 screen, along with a couple of hundred other assorted humans, while my left hand and mind are giving me images of erotic intensity enough to blow my head off.

I rub the very tip of each nipple in turn, using the end of my middle finger. My finger sends messages direct to my vulva which is swelling so hard I can scarcely contain it. Rachel's body is rigid with concentration. A swift glance at her eyes shows she is lost inside her imagination, every thought and nerve-ending concentrated on that one spot. Her mouth has opened slightly, there is saliva gleaming on her teeth and the edge of her tongue.

I press, quickly and a little hard. She lets out a little gasp, tries to smile at me, but loses her breath as I butterfly my fingers round the thrusting nipples, tracing the swollen ridges on what I know to be pale biscuit-coloured rings.

I take my hand away from her skin, lifting the weight of the warm satin and wool and trace a line with my index finger from below her breasts to her waistline, follow along the crevice of her waist, down to her navel. Feather round it. Yes, she's naked here, too. I am both light- and heavy-headed with excitement.

I spread my hand over her hot belly, pointing my middle finger down to the crisp, curling nest. She gasps again as I run all my fingers down over her mons. I rub my garnet ring along the place where her thigh folds up against her belly, push my little finger between her furry lips. She is hot and wet. I draw some of her juice up onto her nipples, bend them gently back and forth. She is beginning to shift in her seat. I am not sure how long I can control my breathing and the desire to make some noise.

I push my hand down between her legs so that my middle finger can rub against the taut magenta muscle between her vulva and her anus. She is nearly lifting out of her seat and suddenly rasps, 'Could we go, please?'

I stumble to my feet, scrabbling for my coat and the bag of food, trampling on many disapproving toes on my way to the aisle. Rachel is ahead of me, and thrusting through the emergency exit doors. As she turns the corner of the corridor I catch up with her, drop my coat and the feast, take her by the shoulders and push her up against the wall.

The light here is dim and red. Her eyes are enormous, her mouth open and ripe as a gooseberry. I kiss her very deliberately, very deep. She slips down the wall a little.

I rip open two buttons of her cape and plunge both hands inside, run them over her body from throat to thigh, finally pushing her legs apart and letting my fingers into that hot, wet, slippery cave. Her clitoris is hard and she gasps and shudders as I draw my hand back and forth, back and forth over her swelling, urgent flesh. I am near collapse myself, but keep her up with one arm round her shoulder as she surges and drenches onto my hand, her whole body softening into mine as she lets out one last whistling cry. Forehead touching forehead, we wait for the turmoil of our bodies to calm a little.

'You idiot.' I laugh into her mouth.

She looks up from under her eyelashes. Her swollen lips begin to curve into a smile of glee.

'Didn't you like my magical mystery tour?'

For an answer, I pull on my coat, take up the crumpled bag of food, take her by the arm and guide her outside. Some angel sends a taxi. In the dark warmth of the vehicle we sit innocently enough. The driver can't see my arm sliding into her cape. He probably won't notice the expression of taut-jawed bliss on our faces under the kaleidoscope of lights from passing traffic.

At my flat, I pay the driver off while Rachel goes ahead to open the door. We stumble along the passageway into the central hall. Rachel turns to look at me, opening her arms. The swinging moods, tension and excitement of the last hour or so have taken their toll on me. I feel very much like weeping.

'Put that food down and sit there for a minute,' she orders.

I am only too happy to let her take me over. A few seconds later, she takes my hand and leads me into the bathroom. Water is pouring into the bath, floating Femme into the air. Slowly, carefully, she takes off my coat, shoes and scarf, slides me out of my skirt and blouse, gently disengages my body from my underclothes. Her hands are as careful on me as if I were a baby.

'Have a nice, long, soak,' she says, and disappears.

Relaxed and warm in the bath, I wonder at this woman I am involved with. This whole evening has been an elaborate charade played out for my pleasure. While I was worrying that she might be tired of me, she was planning a marvellous pantomime in which I could play the lead.

It was both a magnificent gesture and a token of affection. She had refuted my suspicions, pledged her attachment to me and given us both exquisite pleasure in one fell swoop.

'Time to come out,' she calls.

Slipping my caftan over my head, I go through to the sitting-room. Rachel is sitting in the middle of a nest of downies. The honeyed glow of candles is flickering over the curves of her soft breast and belly, glittering on bronze hair. She stands up, lifting my caftan as she goes, taking it over my head and throwing it to one side.

'It's your turn now.'

I close my eyes and listen as she takes my breasts in her hands, pulling them gently as if she were plucking fruit. The heat goes lancing down to my vagina, which starts up a slow pulsing. She takes us both down to our knees, licks into my navel, runs her fingers so lightly up my flanks from knee to armpit, cups her hot, hot mouth over each breast in turn, sucking hard, then leaving the electrically charged skin to tingle in the air. I thrust my belly at her and she licks it round and round. I have my legs wide apart to ease the torture of my engorged cunt, wanting, yet not wanting, the release of her touch.

Her body comes against mine and my skin feels taut and sore with the need to have contact with her. My breasts are bursting to fill her mouth. She rises up so that our nipples are brushing, lowers her mouth onto mine. I cling on, desperate to get inside her, have her inside me. My tongue is frantic to show how much I love her.

Pulling my head gently back by the hair, she raises my arm and kisses me deep in my armpit, licking at the damp skin, pressing into the sensitive place where my breast is rooted. The fingers of her other hand begin to stroke my labia. My muscles pulse to pull her in. I want to open up every throbbing nerve end to her. I sink back, my knees flung far apart and offer her my aching body.

She lowers her head and begins to tongue me. I cannot get enough of her mouth. Her tongue is hard, changing shape to fit the curves and aching depths I offer her. Her mouth is pouring saliva into me as I pour love juices out on her. The air is redolent with woman-smell. My whole being is gathered in that central place where her mouth is loving me. When I think I must burst with tension and the need to take her in to me, she begins to push her fingers into my vagina, slowly, slowly, prolonging my desire exquisitely, slowly in and out until I feel the dam begin to break and the waves of heat and loosening follow each other through my pelvis and down my legs. My whole body melts into quiescence.

I come back to myself wrapped warm in Rachel and the downie. She smiles at me as she runs a finger along my mouth.

'Now do you believe I love you? Do you believe I want you as much as you want me?'

I nod my silent gratitude for her gift to me of trust in her and belief in myself.

'So what about some of this?' She sits up, reaches a tray down from the sofa and begins to feed me dripping olives and peppers with her lovely, sticky fingers.

RUSH HOUR WITH RHIANN

LINDA DEVO

Picture this, rush hour on the tube. I came charging down the stairs in my usual manner and just made it through the doors of the train. Here I was crushed between a 'Jack-the-lad' and the doors, my face buried in his moist unsexy-smelling armpit, with nothing to hang onto to stop myself from falling all over the place. I slowly shuffled around to face this gorgeous, dark haired hunk of a woman leaning nonchalantly against the glass partition, looking for all the world like she was on a desert island by herself, instead of on a tightly packed tube in the middle of the rush hour. I was starting to feel hot, not quite sure whether to attribute it to the incredible build up of heat on the train or to this beautiful looking woman.

I looked into her face and got caught staring at her weird, green eyes. She stared back, not batting an eyelid till my eyes watered from the effort to stop myself blinking. She looked away, quietly smirking to herself. She quickly wiped it off her strong features before she looked back at me. She turned around, laughter flickering in her eyes. I looked down feeling completely mortified. The train, by this time, had pulled into several stations, one of them mine. I had this half-witted idea to get off when she did and follow her. Silly, but by this time I was bewitched and I wanted to know who she was, where she was going and who to see.

The train started with a jerk and threw me onto her; I apologized profusely and died a slow death from embarrassment. Left hand holding my bag, I put my other hand on the glass partition she was leaning on, desperately trying to pull together some semblance of dignity and cool. I didn't dare look up at her, instead I concentrated on keeping my balance even though I was effectively propped up by the people around me. I caught myself staring at her breasts, sweet curves visible through her shirt, fantasizing, losing myself in the soft, luscious flesh. I felt a thigh pressing between mine and turning sideways to gain more access, I looked up ready to slap the owner and saw her looking at me. I suppose I looked startled because she laughed, this deep throaty laugh that made all the hairs on the back of my neck stand on end. My legs started to quiver, losing their battle to stay closed and I shifted my footing so her thigh was right between both of mine and pressed my body closer to hers.

Not one word was spoken, we just sort of sidled to the door till we were wedged in the corner. She started to move her thigh, first in barely perceptible circles, then slowly started to gain momentum, her left hand slipping between us towards my cunt, stopping on the way to draw roughly on my nipples. When she moved her hand, I stepped in closer till our nipples were touching lightly, the rocking of the train did the rest. I desperately wanted to kiss her; instead I felt my zipper being tugged downwards and an impatient hand pulling at the waist of my pants. She struggled to get her hand in and succeeded.

The train stopped and we both froze as the man, unknowingly sheltering us, pushed his way out. Horrible visions of us getting caught with her hands down my knickers, getting arrested for public indecency flashed before my eyes. For once, I was glad there were hordes of people waiting to get on the train. I couldn't possibly have stopped her if I wanted to, not that I did.

As the train started to move again, her middle finger started making a path for itself through my damp hairs to my clit. She made it and slid the tip of her finger over it and whispered in my ear,

'Is all this wet for me?'

I didn't dare speak because I knew the words wouldn't come out like they were meant to. I didn't even dare move ... someone might have felt the rhythmic gyrations that had nothing to do with the erratic movement of the train. She slid her thumb up my cunt as far as she could bury it, moving it up and down in a hypnotic movement. It took all my willpower to stop myself from bouncing on it. She pulled her thumb out and started to stroke my clit again with her thumb, two of her fingers still up my cunt. My nerve endings were fit to explode and I started to thrust my cunt at her fingers, all the time staring into her eyes. She whispered again,

'Now babe, come now.'

That did it. My thighs clamped over her hand as I came in long, burning streaks, and all through this she stroked me till I came again with short almost painful bursts. I stood there clutching at her arm, letting a low, guttural moan escape, my legs completely gone. She took her fingers back and raised them to her face as if to scratch her nose, breathed in deeply, mouthed 'Nice' to me, and smiled.

I managed a weak grin back while she pulled a pen out of her back pocket. She took hold of my hand which was still clinging to her arm and wrote on my sweaty palm, 'Maybe you'd like to return the favour sometime, Rhiann,' and scribbled her number underneath the message.

The train stopped and she made to push her way out, threw a backward glance and said,

'Nice meeting you.' She winked, a wicked look glinting in her eyes.

I sunk back into my space, completely oblivious to the curious stares I was getting from my fellow travellers. They all probably thought I was going to faint because of the heat. The bizarreness of the whole episode suddenly struck me and I burst out laughing.

The train pulled into its last stop and everyone got off. I crossed platforms to get the train back to my station, rummaging through my bag for a pen and diary. At least I had the good sense to copy her number out before it was wiped off my sweaty palm. Maybe I would call her soon ... like tonight!

ANEMONE WOMAN

BERTA R FREISTADT

The anemone on my finger
Sucked and sucked
Her fronds waved
As I went by
Attracting me
Her colouring
Flashing at me
Aloof, enticing
Magnetic creature
Octopus then
Arms to hold
To touch, to tease
To reassure
One for each day
Of the week
And some over

And the anemone
Waiting for me
Deep in the sea
Of night

ROTARY SPOKES MEETS TALLULAH THE BAG LADY

FIONA COOPER

'I just want some space,' said Jess distractedly, 'I love you Rotary Spokes, but I need some space!'

Well, shee-it! She could take a hint. All she heard was an echo of her first rejection, Diz the dumb druggie and her cosmic psycho-babble, meaning get out of my life.

That was five weeks ago, and now she was in London. You want some space, Jess, I'll put a goddam ocean between us. Ha! She had done Spats, the Black Cap, Heds, Chain Reaction, every goddam bar and disco in the capital of England, and she'd got just one word for it all: Chickenshit.

She'd been chatted up, propositioned, cold-shouldered, prepositioned, drunk, sober, blind drunk; she'd bopped till she dropped, sat morosely over drinks in dark corners for hours, blinded herself under strobes, deafened herself with trying to talk against the music. And it all seemed pretty pointless.

She mooched out of King's Cross station, bending the steel user-hostile barriers without noticing and strode into the street with no particular place to go. The hookers on the corner looked cold and weary and she wondered what it would be like to go with a hooker. Sheeee-it! She was missing Jess. She ate the ratburger and chips, so re-constituted that they should have been in a goddam museum, not aching their death-throes through her gut. She shrugged through the windows at the off-licence and paid far too much for a bottle of Bourbon. Skid fucking row, she thought, up-ending the bottle in the street. Who gives a flying fuck for when you're down and out.

She slouched off the main drag and found a doorway between boarded-up windows. The bourbon was on its way to half-empty when she heard a voice made up of a rusted American twang, a bronchitic drawl, and a shrill rage all at once.

'Get off my bleedin' patch, you big yobbo!'

She looked up. There stood a squat woman, wild as she was tall. Fringes flew from every surface, feathers around her head shivered in the skulking city breeze. She looked like a pyramid built out of mud by a child, bags spilling string and paper heaped around her feet. Rotary Spokes shifted to one side of the step.

'Join me if you like,' she said, 'I don't get the inclination to move, tell the truth.'

'Shit,' the bag lady spat, 'you don't give a girl a choice, your sort. I remember when there was a bit of respect for age, yeah, age and experience, that meant something at one time, you'd never remember it. I've slept here every night for twenty years, I'll tell you fuck-features, not that you care. I've never yet had to share it. I carry everything I own and ...'

Rotary Spokes handed her the bottle to shut her up.

'I don't drink corn liquor, what do you think I am? Now if you had a little brandy, we're talking.' The voice was suddenly throaty and almost appealing.

'Okay, okay, okay.'

Rotary giggled as she went back to the off-licence. Why the hell not? She bought Armagnac. That should stop her whinging. But the bag lady just looked and snorted contemptuously.

'I never thought you'd come back! Are you nuts? One of those writers doing shit about the real life on the streets? I could tell you stories, but I'm not going to. One of these days, I'll get me a typewriter and put it all down and you won't believe it. And I'll get the money, honey, all of it!'

'I know what you mean,' Rotary growled, 'I had some writer pinch my life and put it in a book a while ago. She's got the goddam fame and fortune and I'm sitting on the motherfuckin' pavement drinking bourbon. All I got is a broken heart.'

'Broken heart?' jeered the bag-lady. 'If that's your only problem, zip your lip round me. You know what I was? 'Course you don't. I was a prima ballerina and if you snigger, I swear I'll break your ass.'

Now, it was a little difficult to imagine this skunk's nest rollerball of motheaten fabrics pirouetting in a tutu, but Rotary Spokes had a reverence for all forms of life and didn't even smile.

'Yeah, I'm down on my luck,' slurred the bag-lady, gulping brandy. 'I could have been Pavlova if I'd been Russian. I was born too late and in the wrong place. Rail-roaded out of Shitsville, Massachussetts, and I've been on the road ever since. I've done every kind of dancing; supper shows, night-clubs, everything.'

Rotary was not aware of a Ballet de Shitsville. But Jess had always told her she had no culture, so she made no comment. And whether it was the bourbon or the full moon overhead or just that she'd had England and the English up to her eyeballs, she made a decision.

'I gotta go,' she said. 'If you'd like to come to my place, we could drink the rest of this in more accomodatin' surrounds.'

'Okay,' said the bag-lady. Was it a trick of the light or did her eyes suddenly hold a certain gleam? Rotary Spokes felt a certain stirring deep in her half-sozzled guts.

It was a helluva job getting the bag-lady into a taxi. Not just her girth but the fuckin' British attitude of the first seven taxi-drivers.

'Cock-sucking snobs!' taunted the bag-lady.

Finally they reached the hotel. Rotary glanced at the desk-clerk and swaggered over to the lift, carrying half the bag-lady's possessions, only relinquished when she assured her that it would be a real honour. Two deficentos in evening wear declined to ride in the same lift, so when they reached her floor, Rotary jammed the doors open with the nearest laundry basket. Let the assholes walk!

'Is this a palace or what?'

The bag-lady shambled round the room, opening the doors, running the taps, flushing the toilet and finally, she picked up the phone.

'I've seen it in the movies!' she hissed, then screeched: 'Room Service? I want a champagne supper for two. NOW!'

'Is champagne alright with you?' she said, slamming the phone down. Rotary Spokes collapsed across the bed, giggling.

'Just fine,' she said.

'I'm going to freshen up a little,' said the bag-lady, with a glare.

She peeled off her bedraggled, moss-green outercoat and dropped it on the floor. Next went an outsize cardigan, which might have been grey at some point. She unpinned her skirt. Rather, her top skirt. Then the next skirt. And then a series of shirts, tattered colours like a city river and about as appealing to the nostrils.

'You like watching a woman taking her clothes off?' she snarled.

'Yiz, I do,' said Rotary Spokes. 'You ain't the same shape as I thought.'

'I've forgotten what shape I am,' the bag-lady grumbled, 'I don't have many engagements these days. And there's no point in putting all the goods in the shop window, eh, dearie?'

Two inches of bourbon later, there was a shifting mountain of clothes and a pile of safety-pins on the floor. The bag-lady was down to an elaborately lacey slip, clinging to what looked like a very lovely body. And of course, her squashed-grape beret with it's tattered blooms spiking out like a hedgehogs bristles. She smiled for the first time and it was a very inviting smile, a bit uncertain and obviously not much in use. Rotary smiled back.

'You wanna wash my back?' said the bag-lady, fluttering her eyelashes.

Waaall, maybe she was crazy, maybe she had been a ballerina, maybe Rotary Spokes was hallucinating, but this bag-lady, whatever else she was, was a professional flirt for sure.

'Sure.'

And she looked even better in the bath. She'd poured every courtesy sachet of bubble-bath into the water and the foam rose around her naked body. Rotary didn't like to mention the beret. Maybe she never took it off. Folk had a right to do what they needed. She soaked the flannel and ran it over the grimy back.

'Nice. Real nice.' said the bag-lady, throatily, winking and up-ending the brandy bottle.

'You wanna wash your hair?'

'Nah!' the bag-lady grimaced. 'See, honey, if I let my hair down ... I let my hair down. If you know what I mean.'

Rotary Spokes got the full benefit of slate-gray eyes twinkling with no uncertain meaning. Well now ...

'You wanna let you hair down, it's fine by me,' she said, trying to be nonchalant. The bag-lady gazed at her and raised her arms with all the grace of a dancer. She unskewered the battered beret, twirled it on one finger and flung it across the bathroom. Her hair tumbled around her face. It was faded gold, grease-dark at the roots and a tumbled cloud of silver at her temples.

'Beautiful hair,' said Rotary Spokes, catching her breath.

The bag-lady slid backwards in the water and her hair streamed around her like feather-fine, exotic sea-weed. She grabbed the shampoo bottle, *Coral Tips,* and sniffed at it.

'I don't like this brand,' she said, arching an eyebrow.

'I got my own. You kin borrow it if you want.'

Rotary Spokes had a very classy range of toiletries. Everything had to come from Paris, France, ever since the Phoenix of Texas. The bag-lady okayed the shampoo and worked her incredibly long hair into a thick plume of white cream. She was really quite a looker, when you got down to it. And of all the places you really can get down to it, a bath-tub is one.

'Mind if I smoke?' said Rotary Spokes.

'I'll join you,' said the bag-lady, drying one hand and taking the lit cigarette.

'I'll get an ashtray,' said Rotary Spokes and went into the other room. Jesus, those clothes had a life of their own! She caught sight of herself in the mirror and grinned. Hmmm. Maybe London wasn't so chickenshit after all.

In the bathroom they finished their cigarettes and Rotary found a use for the huge flowered jug she'd thought of as a cissy English ornament till now. Clear water streamed the foam from the bag-lady's hair and she rose like Venus from the waves. Rotary caught her breath. The bag-lady looked at her in no uncertain way through her eyelashes ands stepped into the huge towelling robe and padded through to the bedroom.

'Waste not, want not,' she mumbled and dumped all her clothes into the tub. Time enough in the morning to think what the hotel staff would say, thought Rotary Spokes, then started as there came a knock at the door

The bell-hop was standing there, holding a tray that looked like something out of Dallas. She sealed his grin to marble terror with a glare, signed the slip and brought in their late night supper.

Sheee-it! The bag-lady was sitting up in the ridiculously wide bed, a knowing look, a towel on her head like a turban and not a stitch else in sight.

'I was going to say, let's have breakfast in bed,' she said, smokily, 'only, it's not breakfast time. Yet. Get your clothes off, honey, and come in here.'

Well, what's a girl to do? Rotary Spokes undid her shirt, button by button.

'Don't rush,' purred the extraordinary voice, 'I like to watch too, you know.'

Rotary Spokes blushed and undid her belt. Then her fly buttons. The bag-lady was smiling through the smoke of her cigarette. Rotary shucked off one boot and let it drop. Then the next. She pulled off her jeans and stood naked except for her silk boxers.

'Mm — very nice,' said the bag-lady, tossing her soaking turban to the floor. 'Just pick up that champagne, honey, drop your drawers and get over here.'

Well, how lovely. Iced champagne in one hand and the other on the soft heat of the bag-lady's shoulders, the damp fluffiness of her hair steaming an expensive perfume. How very lovely.

The bag-lady picked up a chicken leg and stripped it to the bone with her apple-white teeth. She curled her foot around Rotary's calf. She downed a half-dozen oysters and her toes idly massaged Rotary's thigh. Rotary lifted the silver lid from the last dish. She ripped the shell from a lobster and fed strips of it to the pouting lips shimmering beside her. The bag-lady returned the compliment, then swept the dishes to the floor and knelt over Rotary Spokes.

'You got lobster on your cheek, honey,' she said and licked it off.

'Waaall, I sure ain't got lobster all over my face,' thought Rotary, 'mm, still less on my neck. And I never have been a woman to dip her breasts into her food ...'

She ran her fingers through the damp mane moving tenderly around her nipples.

'I'm a little out of practise, honey,' said the lovely mouth into her midriff.

Rotary tossed a lobster claw onto the floor and snuggled deep down under the duvet. It was wonderful there in the dark, her fingers exploring the soft warmth of this stranger's skin.

'I gotta call you something,' she said, as her hand erupted on a voluptuous breast. The bag-lady shot upright.

'I thought anonymous sex was the thing these days,' she said, obviously flustered and reaching for more champagne. 'You don't have to be polite to me. I've read about it, well, half an article in some goddam newspaper one night when I couldn't sleep.'

'I don't go for anonymous sex,' said Rotary Spokes, 'and I don't never just be polite, you know?'

Her strong arm was around the bag-lady's shoulders and one huge hand was getting into serious appreciation of the third softest area of skin on a woman's body; a quiescent, gently throbbing nipple.

'You can call me Tallulah,' said the bag-lady. 'I've always liked that name.'

'Waaall, thank you,' said Rotary Spokes, 'I'm Rotary. I do got another name, only I'll have to whisper it, cuz I'm shy.'

'Blow in my ear and I'll follow you anywhere!' said Tallulah, wriggling her body right against Rotary's lean, muscled length.

Now, for a woman who claimed to be out of practise, Tallulah was amazingly inventive and agile. Just as Rotary was getting used to exploring the soft suck and bite of her lips, her head ducked away and her hair was flowing over Rotary's belly, her mouth teasing great, gentle bites from her spine and the dip in her back, red-hot kisses rained like lava on her thighs and knees ... her hands coaxed shuddering sighs from her dizzy head and her mind was filled with a huge technicolour screen tumbling with oceans and waterfalls.

'You first,' said Tallulah, firmly, and pinned one radiant arm across her quivering belly. Her hands butterflied over the skin burning between her thighs and she coaxed her fingers through the soaking curls of dark hair to where Rotary's cunt was singing her need and desire. But her fingers were just the heralds for her regal mouth, her soft lips found their place.

Oh, die and go to heaven! Her lips parted and the fluid heat of saliva and tongue met the purple rose petals flooded with ecstasy, her tongue and teeth soldered themselves against her cunt, a playful finger twirled tentatively, then surely, into her ass.

Rotary Spokes became the milky way gone nova. Tallulah the Bag-Lady went into orbit until she was the Seven Sisters in a meteor shower, exploding into the aurora borealis.

Midday, the next day, Tallulah said:

'I got places to walk to. You wanna walk with me?'

'I aint much fun walkin', honey, but ...'

'I don't want to ride in a car!' said the bag-lady. 'I hate cars. You can't breathe. Now, if you had a *bike* ...'

'Waaall, it just so happens ...' said Rotary Spokes. She picked up the phone. 'Could you prepare my bill? I'm checkin'out.'

She crushed the bag-lady to her and kissed her like the four minute warning had just sounded. They kissed till well past the all-clear. Tallulah stretched like Dame Margot Fonteyn.

'Honey,' she said, 'we got places to go.'

UNTITLED POEM I

STORME WEBBER

the golden light behind yr eyes
looking into me
on nights like these
if i were the wolf
i feel inside
i'd find a solitary hillside
fling back my head
& moan a long low one
for you
my love

UPSTAIRS THERE IS A ROOM WITH A BED

INGRID MACDONALD

It's six pm on a Friday and I'm finishing the last of a thousand calls I swear I've made this week. I should have known better about this job. 'The glamorous world of advertising', the ad in the *Globe and Mail* had said. 'Are you creative, good with people and looking for the challenge of your life?' That was two years ago — and I fell for it. Now I feel surgically attached to a telephone, wasting the best years of my life on cranky, tight-fisted customers. Some glamorous world.

I'm trying to wrap up my last call — the one to the carpet-cleaning company — when the highlight of my week, probably the highlight of my life, walks in, dangling her car keys. I wave and gesture that I'll be just a second. She sidles up to me and writes a cute, little note: 'Jingling of keys means get off the phone, leave crummy office and come with me for a weekend of wild sex.' She jingles fiercely.

Now, in my own defence, let me say that I am trying to get off the phone. I want to, really, but I have to be nice to the carpet-cleaning lady and sometimes I just don't know how to say goodbye. I scribble back, 'Justa sec.' She looks at me in disbelief, then smirks and jangles her keys loudly into the receiver.

'Is that your other phone?' the carpet-cleaner lady asks uncertainly.

'Phone?' The phones in our office beep rather than ring but she doesn't need to know that. 'Yes. My goodness, my other line. Shall I call you first thing Monday?' and I try to ring off: 'Uh-huh, yes ... Okay ... Is that so? ... Yes, you too, 'bye now ... right ... uh-huh. Goodbye,' I say finally and hang up.

'Well, that's done. Hi Cheryl, how's my baby?'

'Ready to go,' she says.

'So am I. Here's our groceries for the weekend. Here's my suitcase of old clothes. Here's that terrible novel I borrowed from you last week. And here's what's left of me, ready to eat you up.'

'All for me? I must have been a good girl,' she smiles coyly. 'You look beautiful. I want to kiss you.'

'Wait until we get to the car, my love,' I say, hurrying her towards the elevator. I'm dying to kiss her as we sprint across the underground parking-lot at a quick pace. In the car we kiss a long time, until we've had enough to last the hour's drive north.

'You could have warned me about the book,' I say.

'You didn't like it? But it's a classic.'

'*Closetted Woman Kills Self In Anguish Over Lesbian Passion.* A bit tragic for my tastes.'

'Sylvana, it's literature. Hélène Robichaud is a brilliant writer. *Time* magazine called her a genius.'

'If she really was a genius, she could have racked her immense brain and come up with a happy ending.'

'You're such a philistine sometimes. Hélène Robichaud is writing the true story of her friend Rebekah, whose family ostracized her when they found out about her 'abnormal passions'. They wanted to institutionalize her for being a lesbian, so she drowned herself in a gesture of freedom. That was the only way she felt she could have control of her own destiny.'

Freedom in drownings. Glamour in advertising. Help me, St Teresa, I'm losing track here on earth.

'I know what you're saying, love, but it upsets me. The book is so claustrophobic. I wanted there to be a way out that wasn't jumping down a well.'

'Sometimes there is, sometimes there isn't. You're forgetting how much has changed for lesbians in the past twenty years. And maybe Robichaud wrote a depressing story on purpose, so that the reader would know what it was like to be a lesbian in a repressed culture.'

'Depressing people on purpose. Is that post-modern?'

But Cheryl doesn't answer. She jams her foot on the accelerator and speeds the car up the parkway.

While she drives, I lean back and admire — the view and her. Cheryl likes to drive. It gives her a feeling of smooth control in a rapidly changing world. Sometimes she likes to talk. She talks mostly about her ideas, and about the details of her other lives, of which she has two. I rank third in her personal hierarchy and get to see her one day a week. Her live-in lover, Rita, is in a constant battle for first place with Cheryl's work as a chiropractor.

After a while, I notice Cheryl hasn't mentioned Rita yet. This means bad news. Casually I venture, 'And how's Rita these days?'

Cheryl shoots me a look. A wince.

'It was a struggle to get this weekend, that's for sure. She was sobbing on the couch when I left. It'll be a long time before we can do this again, I just want you to know.'

I can tell by the tone of her voice that she's being euphemistic. 'A struggle' probably meant several hours of shouting and throwing things. Rita's not really big on Cheryl spending too much time with me, ever. I'm not much help either. If I call their house and Rita answers, I hang up. Rita always knows it's me, too, which makes it worse. Several times Cheryl has patiently explained to me that it would be much better if I would just politely ask to speak to her. And I try, but I panic. I feel like such a kid. Every time I ask about Rita, I half hope that Cheryl will say that Rita has taken a job with an arctic research group, and leaves for Yellowknife tomorrow.

At least I know better than to pursue this one. There have been times when I have pathetically begged Cheryl to leave Rita and devote herself to me. Each time, she flatly refused. Those conversations sit in my conscience as ugly disasters. Today, I let the topic slide. Besides, we got this weekend, which is what we wanted. What I wanted.

It is dusk as I give Cheryl the last few instructions to the farmhouse drive. Getting out of the car, I think how wonderful it would be if Cheryl and I were arriving here to live. I could leave the ad job, she could leave her chiropractic patients, we could both leave Rita far behind us, in the city. We could be in love all day and every day.

Wishing makes me silly with happiness. I rush over to Cheryl and grab her hand,

'Well? Do you like our new home? Isn't it wonderful?'

She hugs me, laughing. At least she likes my sense of humour.

'I'll have to show you the orchard. It's so beautiful.'

I pull her around to the back of the house where the ground is bumpy with rust-coloured balls of fallen apples. The grass smells musty and sweet. The late afternoon light turns her face a dark bronze. The sun turns the drying corn stalks to gold. The soil is black with humus where the tractors have turned it for fall. I am happy.

Inside, I show her the wood piled by the stove, the pantry full of the season's yield; peaches, pickles, berries — and goods from the farmer's market; olives, herring, rounds of cheese, vinegar, three kinds of oil, long braids of garlic. I have brought fresh pasta, bread and a jar of home-made sauce. I want to assure her that she will want for nothing, that we'll be content for the rest of our lives, or at least for the weekend. I want her to have a sense of harvest, that there is plenty of everything.

This is such a departure for us. We're used to suffering the restraints of forbidden love. Hasty sex, one day a week, and days on end when we are unable to meet or speak. In the city, at my apartment, we've barely finished making love before she's rolling over and getting dressed again.

'What are you doing?' I ask, incredulous.

'It's nine-thirty. I said I'd be home.'

'But how can you walk?'

Then I'm courteous in a way that I know hurts her, showing her the door offering her a cheek to kiss goodbye.

'Don't,' she says.

'"Don't" what?' I say and say good night and cry until I fall asleep.

I offer to make some food, though I know it's not food she wants. She smiles and says,

'Not just now.'

She is still smiling as I take her hand and lead her upstairs.

◆ ◆ ◆

Upstairs, there is a room with a bed. Decorated by my mother, I have left it untouched since my girlhood. I can be so sentimental, it pains me at times. On the wall are pictures of animals (cat family) and of the Blessed Virgin Mary (holy family). On the bed are pillows in hand-crocheted coverings and dolls with glass eyes.

In my tailored suit, I seem large and unlikely in such a nostalgic room. But I have chosen not to change the decoration. I rarely visit my mother and often miss her. She doesn't live that far away from the farmhouse and sometimes I hope she'll drop by.

Cheryl laughs. 'This is pretty lady-like for a butch like you, Manino.'

'Too bad you love it, Shablynski.'

'You're right I do,' she says crossing the room. She kisses me and starts to undo the buttons on my shirt.

When we begin, I always want to make love to her first. I'm electric with hunger, afraid I won't be able to fill the emptiness inside me. I feel her heavy breasts under her layers of clothes. I stroke them, feeling for the hardening nipples as she makes wonderful noise. Her kisses become harder. My hands move up and down the length of her back, around the sides of her body, returning again and again to her wonderful breasts. I bring my lips to hers and softly, softly smooth her forehead and cheeks, feeling for the small hairs that cover her skin. Then I hold the back of her head with my palms and kiss her long and hard.

She is pulling off my clothes now, slipping my jacket to the floor. When she goes for my belt buckle, I move her hands away and help her off with her clothes instead. Then I throw open the bed clothes and pause for the slightest second to arrange the pillows for her head. She leans back. I tease her with the fabric of my pants against her skin. She grabs for my nipples through my unbuttoned shirt, sucking one while pulling the other with a furled hand. Her eyes are closed and I feel intense emotion coming off her in waves, like a kind of heat. I hold her tight, kissing her.

Reaching down, I find the handful of warm wetness and the sopping lips of her cunt. My hand caresses the folds, holding off for just a moment to let her pleasure rise before I safely, safely slip on a translucent rubber glove and dab a drop of jelly on my fingers. As I go in with two fingers, she moans and breathes deeply. She makes these high, effluent, whinnying sounds. I kiss her, making my mouth hollow and round; she pushes her tongue in and out. I am watching her intently as I move more fingers into her cunt. I ease, with careful persistence, down the warm glove of her vagina, until all my five fingers are curled tightly into her. I feel the back of my hand against the base of her cunt, my fingertips arch to feel her smooth front wall, the back of my fingers feel the soft knob of her cervix. I have slipped one arm under her neck to hold her firmly, lovingly, while I rock my hand inside her, drawing it in and out to the rhythm of her breath. I can tell by her voice that she is far away and given over to pleasure. The slightest movement sends her deep into pleasure. I fuck her this gently until she lets me know she has had enough.

I take my hand out — slowly unwinding it. Her clit needs only to be breathed on and she's alive with feeling, inhaling and shuddering as I stroke her, brushing my hands across her clit, now large and pink and hard in her glistening lips. Holding her, watching her, I am overwhelmed with awe. Listening to her tight rapid breaths, I touch her clit with long strokes. She gasps and folds her legs across my hand to hold it, then she gasps again and lets go. For a long time after that I hold her, caressing her face until we fall asleep.

◆ ◆ ◆

The sound of a car coming up the driveway wakes us. We are both naked under the covers and the morning is dazzling and bright. Sun streams through the lace-covered windows. A car horn honks.

'Who could that be?' I wonder, putting on a robe and moving to the window, shielding my eyes from the brightness. 'Oh my god,' I say, looking out and recognizing the woman getting out of the car below. I open the window.

Cheryl is suddenly awake. 'Who is it?'

'It's my mother.'

'Your mother?' She looks at the clock. 'Does she always visit at eight o'clock on Saturday mornings?'

'She never comes here. This must be the first time in five years that she's shown up.'

'What should I do? Should I hide?'

'Not at all. Don't worry, she'll love you. I told her all about you on the phone.'

'You told her about me?' Cheryl is aghast. 'What did you tell her? That you're sleeping with a lapsed-Catholic adulteress? Oh my god Sylvana I can't believe it. I'm naked in your bed and your mother is in the driveway.'

'Will you relax?' I lean out of the window, 'Hi Ma, how ya been doing? Did you bring eggs? That's so thoughtful of you.'

My mother is wearing a beige linen dress that she made herself. She's all radiant, what with the sun and the linen and the shining mists.

She shouts up, waving, 'Hi Sylvana. How's my little girl? Being good? Your father was asking last night how you were. I thought I'd come over to see if you were around.'

'I'm great Ma. You look beautiful, I gotta tell ya.'

'Have you got someone up there with you, Sylvana?'

I grin sheepishly, 'Yeah.'

'I can always tell when you are with someone. Is it the one with the other girlfriend?'

'That's the one. Her name is Cheryl, Ma, I told you before.'

'Oh yeah, Cheryl. You tell her to come to the window. I want to talk to her.' I turn back to the room. Cheryl is sitting with the sheet wrapped over her breasts. She looks like she has been trying not to breathe.

'Cher, my mom wants to talk to you.'

'To me? What does she want to talk to me about? Tell her I'm not dressed yet. Tell her I'm asleep.'

'I can't say that, it would hurt her feelings. Just talk to her a bit.'

'Okay,' she groans and reluctantly shuffles to the window in her bed sheet. 'Hello Mrs Manino, a beautiful morning today.'

'Hello there Cheryl. Now listen, do you love my daughter?'

Speechless, Cheryl turns back to me , 'What should I say?' Her eyes are wild with surprise.

'Just answer her. Tell her the truth.'

'Oh that.' Cheryl wrinkles her nose for a second and sticks her head out the window again. Clutching her sheet she says, 'Yes, I do love your daughter. Very much so, Mrs Manino.'

'But you've got all those troubles with the other girlfriend all the time, yes?'

'Well not all the time. It's not always easy if that's what you mean.'

'And Sylvana, she makes you happy, doesn't she? I mean she's a nice girl, and she works hard, and she has that glamorous job in advertising, and she makes you feel good. Yes?'

'Well, yes. I love being with her when I can.'

'So why don't you leave that other woman and be with Sylvana? She gets so upset when you're not around. Sometimes she calls me and oh, she cries and cries.'

'I've never thought of it that it way before, Mrs Manino. You mean I should just leave Rita and take Sylvana as my lover and forget this once a week business?'

'That's right.'

'Okay, well now that we've talked about it, that seems like a good idea. I'll do that then. Just let me tell Sylvana.

◆ ◆ ◆

When Cheryl turned back to the room I was asleep. She said,

'Sylvana. Sylvana. Honey.'

I woke up to the dazzling white sun streaming through the lace behind Cheryl's back. 'Syl, there's a woman in the driveway.'

I was groggy with sleep. 'What does she look like?'

'I don't know. Older. Wearing a flowered dress and an apron.'

I put on my robe and looked out but it was only Mrs Grodin bringing the milk. I leaned out,

'Thank you Mrs Grodin, just leave it on the steps and I'll pay you Sunday.'

She nodded and the bottles clinked down. I stood watching out the window as she drove away. Cheryl put her arms around me from behind. I could feel her breasts and her belly, their warmth against the silk of my robe.

SONNET GOLD AND BRONZE

JEWELLE GOMEZ

You rise above me on the hard wood floor
Your eyes turn from hazel to thunder
The gold of you is translucent,
eclipsing the movement of your body over mine;
firm, sporting legs and belly against my pliancy.
We are hiding deep inside
but the wood against my back makes me forgetful.
I fold you inward like a puzzle
and believe to hide is all we have.

I am dark, copper earth gone bronze.
Your breath warming my skin
makes me come.
Your hand inside reaches up
to expose me inside out.

KID'S STUFF

LIANN SNOW

I was nine and my little sister seven, when they sent us away from home. Our mother was in the latter stages of pregnancy and we were to stay with an aunt in another county until the new baby was born. Our mother had often miscarried, but they thought that this time all would be well.

Auntie Marge was my mother's oldest sister. She was kind, careless, and wryly sarcastic. She called me 'Sunshine', because I was so grave, though she called my sister Hilary by her given name. Except when she ate, a cigarette hung from Auntie Marge's lips and she had to screw up her eyes from the smoke. Even when she bathed her baby son, ashes floated in the tub. She was scruffy and witty, and she loved us uncritically.

We hardly understood why we were not at home, but we were confident that in good time they would come for us and, until then, for those few weeks in that hot, dusty summer, it was a holiday.

At the bottom of the street where Auntie Marge lived, there was a patch of waste ground cut across by a narrow canal. A wooden board on a pole told anyone who could read it that entry was 'prohibited', but the fence was broken so we trespassed heedlessly, along with the local kids.

Strewn across that bumpy, rutted land were some pipes as high as us, and through them we crawled and ran and shouted and sang, delighting in the echoes. Some of the boys and girls did other quieter things, but I stood apart from that, and my little sister stood with me.

Sometimes the water beckoned us. We paddled in it up to our shins while the sun beat down on us, darkening our bodies and lightening our hair.

We got wet and we got dirty, but Auntie Marge did not reproach us. She just laughed and cleaned us and gave us orange juice and comic books, and when the purple evening came, she sent us off 'up the wooden hill' to sleep (as far apart as space allowed) in the old iron bed.

One light-blue morning, after our breakfast of bacon and eggs, we clambered down from the table and clattered out through the dark hallway, eager to play. Auntie Marge called out to me as I reached the front door.

I looked back at her as she stood in the hall holding a red-checked cloth. She had decided it was time I 'lent a hand'.

As I went back into the kitchen to dry up the breakfast dishes, my little sister slipped out into the sun ahead of me.

When I had finished, I folded up the cloth as neatly as I could and asked if I might go out now. She was lighting a fresh cigarette. She coughed before she answered. I saw tears in her eyes. When she said 'Yes', I went out quietly, just in case she changed her mind.

Little Hilary was across the street with some children that I did not know: a big girl, older than me, and some other, smaller kids.

I went over. Hopscotch squares were chalked on the pavement. Some of the little ones were taking turns at it. My little sister was standing watching them. The big girl was beside her. I went up to them.

The big girl stared at me. 'Who are you?' she said.

'This is my sister,' Hilary replied. She seemed glad I had arrived.

I told the girl my name and where we lived and where our auntie lived and a bit about our mother (as much as I knew). She didn't seem very interested.

'I'm Mary,' she said.

She was big ... and old. I thought she was twelve at least. She was taller than me, but she was plain. Her eyebrows grew together in the middle. She looked very fierce. I hoped she wasn't going to fight me. I wondered why she was not at school. Then I remembered it was Sunday. That was why there weren't any cars in the street. Or grown-ups. Just us kids.

We played hopscotch for a while and then 'Please-Mister-Crocodile-May-We-Cross-The-Water?' When Mary was the Crocodile, Hilary had to show her knickers to prove she had yellow on. And we played 'What's The Time Mister Wolf?', and the little kids frightened themselves and screamed, and their voices echoed in the empty, sunny street.

Mary must have got tired of that because she said to me, 'Do you want to see my house?' And I said, 'Yes,' although I hoped it wasn't far.

It wasn't. Just four houses along, diagonally across from Auntie Marge's. It was a terrace house with shallow steps up to the front door. There was a little yard in front, concrete-floored with a low wall separating it from the pavement and another dividing-wall between it and next-door's yard.

I was impressed. My Auntie's house did not have a yard; the front door opened straight onto the pavement. I noticed though, that the front door of Mary's house was not freshly painted like Auntie Marge's was. That made me feel a bit better.

The little kids had followed us to Mary's house, and now, giggling and chattering, they rushed ahead of us and into the yard, where they swirled and whirled like a flock of sparrows, before settling down, kneeling, sitting or squatting on the dusty, cracked concrete.

Hilary and I stood by the steps.

I thought Mary was going to take us into her house, but she just went and stood in the yard.

The little kids were quiet now. They had wriggled themselves into a row with their backs against the wall. Their faces were very shiny and pink and looked very solemn.

Hilary still stood with me for moment, then she turned away and walked into the yard. There was space left at the far end of the row. Hilary sat down there, next to a grubby little boy.

I waited a moment longer, then I went into the yard too, and sat down next to my little sister, squeezing into the corner of the two low walls. I felt the rough brick in the small of my back.

Mary was the only one still standing.

She looked even taller now. I was afraid, but curious. She was so still.

I watched her covertly. Her clothes were much mended, I could see that now. Her ankle socks and sandals were dirty. Her lank dark hair was pinned at one side with a blue plastic slide. I looked for expression on her broad, plain face, but found none.

Abruptly, she moved off across the yard to my right. There was complete silence. I clasped my hands in my lap. My hands were sticky and hot. Then, a sound. A little cry and then giggling and murmuring. I couldn't make out what was said, but I could hear that it wasn't her talking. It was one of the little kids. I wanted to look, but couldn't without craning my neck, so I stared down at the concrete on which I sat. Then I fixed my gaze on my feet splayed out in front of me, and the white dust on my sandals.

Now the giggling and the small odd murmurings were coming nearer.

I sat stiller than a statue, utterly rigid. My hands seemed glued to each other in my lap.

Mary was almost here.

She hung over my little sister, and Hilary wriggled and chuckled while I sat stony. Only my eyes moved.

Then she was here. She was so big. And she leaned over me and crouched and her face was like the moon, and she crumpled up my skirt and lifted me a little so that she could slip her hand under me. Her face was pink and shiny and damp-looking and she did not speak. Her hands were thick and there was dirt under her nails and she undid the buttons of my blouse and put her hands on me. And I said nothing, nor giggled, nor laughed. I just let her.

Then I heard the other kids fidgetting and squealing and she took her hands away and went to quiet them. She returned and knelt beside me. And this time I opened my clothes; and this time I raised myself; and this time I opened my legs for her. And the children chattered and whispered and giggled and fidgetted but she didn't go away. Because I was the one who didn't laugh and I was the one who took her hand and put it where I wanted it.

And the little children sat in the yard and I didn't hear them anymore.

◆ ◆ ◆

Months later Hilary and I went back to our Auntie's house. The whole family travelled down: our mum, our dad, our new baby sister and the two of us. All our relatives from that part of the world came over to Auntie Marge's. They wanted to congratulate our mother on having the new baby. In the middle of the celebrations, when we could hardly hear ourselves think for all the chattering and laughing, Auntie Marge managed to make out a knock at the front door. She came back looking worried.

'It's for you,' she told me. 'Someone called Mary. Asking if you want to play out.'

My heart nearly stopped.

'I don't know her,' I said, shooting a warning look across at Hilary.

Auntie Marge frowned, but went back out to the front door.

And Mary went away.

MISS FROBISHER'S DREAM

ROSIE CULLEN

Gwen took a long hard drag on her cigarette before stubbing it out underfoot. As her bulk shifted the chair creaked ominously; it was an old and flimsy chair, unused to carrying so voluptuous a rear end. Gwen looked about the shed. It was littered with the flotsam and jetsam of generations of sea battered ferrymen. A tap dripped and a leaking pipe contributed to the stinking pool of effluence in the far corner. There was little to interest or disturb Gwen. She groped about in her voluminous carrier bag and happened on a half eaten packet of marshmallow biscuits. The marshmallow sank between her teeth and she felt peculiarly content.

Vera was feeling extremely annoyed. Her schedule for the entire evening lay in tatters. The home cooked dinner at Mrs Bennett's guest house. A passable string quartet at the Freemason's Hall, playing her favourite Sibelius of all things. A last stroll along the shore and bed by eleven with Glynn Powell's 'Birds of the Welsh Coast'. And tomorrow she must drive back to London and prepare for her new position as Deputy Head. Heaven only knew when a replacement ferry would reach them, and really the old man had been quite rude to her she thought. The sun was setting, grotesquely huge and red for a late English summer. Soon it would be dark and the nights were getting chilly. Vera shivered in anticipation as she re-entered the ferryman's cabin.

The woman was there, a blubbering mass of obesity; Vera

flinched with disgust as she watched a marshmallow biscuit being shoved into the grinding mouth, another poised to follow it.

'Really,' Vera thought, 'some people haven't a clue how to look after themselves.'

Gwen smiled generously at the stern looking woman with greying hair, it was in her nature to be friendly, but she could sense that her warmth confused the other woman.

Vera felt disconcerted by this woman, who was not only grossly overweight but grubby too. Vera noted her lank and greasy hair framing smudged cheeks, her too tight floral dress faded and greying, a stain of brown sauce dribbled over her bosom, hem riding up to reveal massive thighs, yellow with old bruises, which puckered and dimpled as she wobbled on the rickety old chair.

Vera stood erect, as she always did, and coughed to draw the woman's attention.

'I've spoken to the man, he's radioed to the mainland and they'll be sending out a replacement ferry as soon as possible.' Vera informed authoritatively. 'In the meantime I suggest we make ourselves as comfortable as we can, it may be some hours wait.' Vera surveyed the room before her with stiff distaste and looked to the woman for support.

Gwen grinned and proffered the remaining biscuits with a generous nod. 'Before I finish 'em all.'

'No thank you.' Vera refused with an exasperated lift of the eyebrows. 'It's Vera by the way, Vera Frobisher.'

'I'm Gwen, — this is a right bloody mess isn't it?'

'Well, it certainly hasn't seen a mop or a duster for many a year.'

'No, I mean the ferry — it'll be after midnight by the time we get back to Manchester and Den's gorra job on tomorow.'

'That's your husband is it?'

'My boyfriend. Him and Wayne have gone off looking for rabbits.'

'Oh.' Vera sniffed, how any man could conceivably choose to date such a slovenly, sluttish creature was beyond her. As usual the thought of sex was disquieting, distasteful, and she wondered why *it* entered her head so insistently, after all she had considered it a thankful release when she and Ann had discontinued their fumblings in the dark and settled for the occassional hug and a goodnight kiss. For a moment Vera envisaged Gwen naked, the massive breasts and bulging stomach as curvacious as one of those ancient goddess figures, repellingly grotesque and yet sensuously appealing. Vera recoiled and felt thankful that Gwen couldn't read her mind.

Gwen wished Vera would sit down and relax instead of hovering in the doorway with an ugly frown on her face. Vera reminded her of a teacher at her son Wayne's school, always organizing, pestering parents, critical of Wayne's lack of progress, a bully. Gwen disliked being bullied, children had bullied her at school because she was fat, teachers had bullied her for being lazy, her mother had scorned her choice of boyfriends, her ex-husband, Bob, had nagged her because she was untidy. Gwen didn't think there was anything wrong with being fat, lazy and untidy, she didn't hurt anyone, it was better than being a dry old stick with a perpetual frown. Gwen lit up another cigarette as Vera pounced on a broom.

'Aha!' exclaimed Vera triumphantly, 'Now we're getting somewhere! If you'd care to brush around I'll find a cloth and ...' Vera turned to find Gwen grinning at her and puffing on a cigarette.

'What's the point?' said Gwen defiantly.

The moon rose, full and bold, but no replacement ferry had appeared. Vera fumed and threatened complaints in higher quarters.

The ferryman merely shrugged, there was a hitch he explained and nothing to be done about it, they must make themselves as comfortable as possible in the shed. Vera snorted, the thought did not entice her. Indeed the very idea of spending the night in that hovel with two men was unnerving.

'Be thankful for small mercies.' Vera reminded herself, with a rueful smile at her choice of adjective, at least she couldn't be molested whilst the woman and her boy were present.

Wayne snuggled closely into the gap between his mother's breasts. He loved the rich, fruity smell of her and the warmth of her capacious body which enfolded his scrawny frame so easily. Wayne sucked his thumb contentedly and drifted into sleep, a sleep hazy with dreams of rolling sand dunes.

Driven indoors by the chill of the night Vera stepped again into the spurious shelter of the cabin. The woman, Gwen, hadn't budged her great bulk but her scruffy little son was now curled in her lap like a stray cat on a welcome bed of straw.

'Really,' Vera thought, 'a boy of that age shouldn't be sucking his thumb.'

The ferryman stood and offered her his chair, and feeling this to be only proper, she accepted. Carefully placing her towel on the rough desk beside her she turned her back on the company and laid her head down with the hope of resting.

Den winked slyly at Gwen and ran his tongue seductively round the edges of his mouth. His action made her chuckle, as he knew it would, a deep gurgling chuckle which always excited him. Gwen attracted men, she drew them to her like bees to a honeypot. They wanted to bury themselves between her huge breasts and dive into her rolls of flesh, bobbing up for air like young children learning to swim. Den was a plumber by trade and he made quips about plumbing her depths, but Gwen's mass would rumble and shake with a laughter as warm and as cruel as the dark abyss of her womb which he could never fill or satisfy. Gwen felt the ache of his desire and smirked as he lit up another cigarette in compensation.

Vera tossed in disgruntled discomfort and caught the look which passed from the boyfriend to Gwen, she recognized that look, it was lust. Only once had she attracted that look to herself, from Sheila, but that was twenty-five, no, twenty-six years ago. It had been a passion which had flared briefly and fiercely, breaking all the rules which Vera had ever known. But Sheila had deserted her, there was someone else, Vera had only been a diversion after all. And Vera, empty, drained and alone had eschewed lust and found comfort at last with Ann, cosy, dependable Ann, with whom sex had become swiftly uninspiring and eventually unnecessary. This woman Gwen reminded Vera of Sheila, not the looks, but something in the eyes, the voracity, that was it. The thought amused Vera as she imagined Gwen gobbling men up into her huge jaws.

Gwen felt her eyelids droop and longed for the luxurious comfort of her bed, her safe haven. It was going to be a long night. She glanced over at Vera, an odd smile was contorting her fine boned face, a face which might once have been attractive, Gwen thought, and still handsome if the woman weren't so tight lipped. Their eyes met and Vera's darted away like an animal disturbed in it's lair. Gwen recognized the look she had caught, she'd seen it many times before; people looked at her body and they thought of sex, men, young or old and sometimes women. Vera was a lesbian, Gwen had assumed that at first glance, sometimes you just know, she mused. Gwen often wondered what it would be like with a woman the notion didn't shock her as it seemed to shock the mothers of Wayne's friends when they read out lesbian scandals in the tabloids. It had never happened of course. Much to the amazement of prettier girls Gwen had always been surrounded by men, men and their lust, and Gwen had been too lazy to take the initiative with any of the women she had fancied.

Gwen appraised Vera afresh; she wondered what Vera might be like behind the frowning exterior if Vera were in love or lust. Would she be tender? Passionate? Would they spend days on end in the sensuous cocoon of Gwen's bed? Stretching and purring like well fed cats? Would Vera's eyes wrinkle up when she laughed, in a way that Gwen knew would make her tingle? Would she whisper seductively in Gwen's ear, dangerous, sexy suggestions? Their eyes met again and the chemistry of the exchange jolted them both.

Gwen was flirting with her! Vera felt sure of it, then floundered and denied the realization almost at once. It was impossible, she was overwrought and tired, her imagination disturbed. As if to put an end to the notion of Gwen making eyes at her, Vera turned away and buried her head into the crook of her arm.

Gwen smiled with pleasure, satisfied with her effect on the other woman. Absently she stroked and twirled the springy curls of her young son's hair. Den and the ferryman were going out for a breather.

Surprisingly, an uneasy sleep came to Vera Frobisher, and disjointed images, halfway to dreaming, drifted across her flickering eyes. She was floating on an enormous pink marshmallow. The sea, a liquid green, lapped gently at the edges and Vera sensed, before she knew, that she was not alone. In the centre of the giant confection lay Gwen, spreadeagled and naked. In the dream Gwen was even larger than in life, each curve curvaciously pronounced. Her nipples, hard and brown, stood out against the softly glowing pink of her skin and the forest of dark hair thatched between her thighs drew Vera's gaze down into the moist cavern within. Gwen chuckled, deep and gurgling, her eyes aglow with desire.

'Come to me!' she sighed, over and over.

And in the dream Vera dared to touch what she could not in life, and all the while Gwen moaned with pleasure and nodded her encouragement. Vera became aware of her own naked body and was not ashamed of it as Gwen enclosed her, kneading into her back with her strong and urgent fingers, sucking at her earlobes and gasping with desire for her, 'Vera!'

'Vera, Vera, — wake up!'

Vera groaned as the pleasure of their encounter coursed through her body and she sank exhausted onto the spongy, powdered softness of the marshmallow. Gwen's arms still clutched about her and her hot breath fanned her face.

'Vera!' Gwen rolled her eyes and shook the old frump. 'It's the ferry — it's here at last.'

Vera blinked and glancing up into Gwen's face pulled her closer, pursing her lips for a kiss.

Gwen chuckled, bemused, 'There now, what have you been dreaming about?' And she hugged Vera to her breast so that the men by the doorway couldn't see that she kissed her.

HOW TO SUCK THEM NECKBONES

TERRI L JEWELL

Them neckbones is something else if done right.
Neckbones cooked in collard greens, in pinto beans
        with bay leaf, onion, cayenne pepper,
you pop them tender neckbones in your mouth
        making sure they ain't too hot,
        ain't too cool to surrender to you.
Play them neckbones like tenor sax,
tease them fibres righteous until slippery.
You gotta entice neckbones with close-mouthed kisses,
        drawing meat slowly toward the throat,
then swallow, assuage the appetite,
        flavor and temptation diving down and down.
You make sure you miss nothing.
Flex the tongue to keep neckbones rolling
        so there ain't no place
        that ain't been persuaded to submit.
Once every dimple, nook and burrow has been plundered,
        nibble and suck, chew and take in
        with final ecstatic motion
until the bone rests juiceless in the mouth.
Then aim your lips for the core, grasp and convince,
        lick and pull until the last lines
        of satisfaction have been spoken.
Yes, them neckbones are something else if eaten proper.

FUCK THE COMPUTER

TINA BAYS

Right now all I want is to see you, be with you, fuck you without anything else except our bodies and imaginations. Why are you thousands of miles away? Instead I'm tapping my desires into the computer and the only response is the glow of words off the screen.

Honey, this is what you do to me, reduce me to fantasies which make me even hotter when I spell them out for you.

◆ ◆ ◆

I've spent a long time getting ready. The more deliberate my preparations, the faster my heart beats. Body slow and soft, heart fast and singing. A warm, oiled bath. Soapy fingers smoothing into crevices. Washing hair, rinsing, clean. Drying off in the small steamy bathroom, rubbing cream into my thighs, my arms, all over, sweet.

In my bedroom, pulling on a clean, silk slip, slightly loose on my body except across the breasts where lace reveals curves and nipples. Rolling on seamed stockings held up by a suspender belt makes my cunt contract; putting on high heels creates a sudden jolt of sex through my belly. An old denim jacket keeps the chill off, and I can't resist my forties hat with the black net veil. Red on my lips, hard, soft, perfume at pulse points, mascara on lashes, never knew the pleasures of all this until I fucked women.

Already squirming in anticipation, cunt swollen and hot. Unable to settle, walking restlessly around my tiny flat, the top of my thighs brush together, the silk of the slip with its insets of rougher lace pull against my body, teasing.

I light candles in all the rooms and am aware of shadows, the smell of hot wax and flowers bought earlier. I want you now, but I have to wait. I can't settle, moving to and fro between my rooms.

Finally a knock. I remember the last time you were here, how I'd had you up against the door, got my hands in your knickers and my fingers in your cunt right there with god knows who walking by a matter of feet away. Will you be in the mood for this surprise? My stomach turns over in nervousness.

You stand there in the open doorway, looking me up and down, then enter into the scene immediately and a slight smirk crosses your face. A frisson of relief waves through me. You step forward, door still open, close but not touching, and trace your fingers across my lips, opening them slightly. Then you reach out and brush lightly across my breasts, slowly back and forth, and my nipples feel as if they're on fire. Already I'm trembling, feel almost faint. We haven't spoken. Our only physical contact is through your hands. It feels like time is locked, standing there, tension zinging back and forth.

And then you push me back, swing the door closed behind you, and turn me round. We're not touching but I stand absolutely still, as you do, the only sound, our breathing. I can't see you, I don't know what you're planning. I can feel the cool air in the hallway on my cunt. It's shocking. I can feel my wetness. My high heels pull the muscles down the backs of my legs and I want to arch my ass back to you. We must touch, now; I'm in danger of losing my cool.

When it becomes even more unbearable you make a move, sliding one arm over my shoulder as the other reaches around my belly. Your hands move over and under, gliding, slipping, and settle on my breasts, teasing my nipples through the slip, circling. grazing and pulling, gently at first and then with more pressure, responding to my pushing with sudden sharpened squeezes which make me gasp.

Now, my head is thrown back, my weight is against you and you're bending to my neck and shoulders, kissing and nipping me. I can't help it, I'm grinding my ass into your cunt, pushing my breasts out to meet your moving fingers.

You turn us both towards the bedroom, and shove us through the door, still connected. I stumble and you hold me up, moving us through the flickering light, turning me yet again so I end up against a waiting wall. You stand back, I stand still, breathing hard, looking at you.

Moving forward, you remove my jacket and brush a slip strap off my shoulder. You contemplate my room, take it in, planning. What's going to happen? I don't care, I do care, I'm running, I'm sinking, I know you can do whatever you want, I can go anywhere.

I can see your face in the candle light, your tall athletic body, your breasts which move softly under a fine cotton shirt. I can smell sex. My body vibrates with desire. I will you to move.

And you do, pulling me away from the wall, snapping the remaining slip strap off my shoulder, exposing my breasts. I sense, rather than see, you reach for a leather belt from the shelf. What's coming? I'm breathless, swooning, thrilled.

Turning me around, you bind my wrists together behind my back and leave me standing there, till you tell me to turn again. Then you lower your mouth to my breasts, sucking the nipples until I'm longing for more, begging, harder, hurt me and finally you bite me and suck and bite again each time creating an electric current through my body. I start to buckle but you catch me and stumble me backwards to the bed, not stopping, easing me falling, back onto the bed.

I lie there, slip in disarray around my hips, still in my stockings, heels and hat. I'm shocked, breathless, exposed. You must fuck me soon.

Not yet. Straddling my body you reach out for the white candle beside the bed and for an instant we stare into each others eyes. Then slowly and deliberately you tip the candle towards my chest. Gasping, I squeeze my eyes shut as you quickly dip another light track of sensation closer to my breasts and finally another which runs across the nipples. Is it hot or cold? I don't know; only that the delicate trail sends showers of tiny explosions to my cunt. I'm writhing with pleasure. I'm blown away by it.

Swinging off me, you roll me over, face down with bound wrists at the small of my back and I lie there, knowing something's to come but not able to see when it will or where you'll choose to decorate. I'm undulating my pelvis uncontrollably into the bed, reaching for the surface with my clit, and then rocking upwards, longing for your touch. I know you can see my cunt, my ass, my back, exposed.

You begin and without the stopping and starting, take me further and further until I'm out of myself, drenched, crying for you.

Suddenly I'm aware that you've paused but there's hardly a moment before you're back, your hands opening my legs wider. I strain upwards, I'm desperate to feel your hand touch my clit, to enter me. Finally, you slide in, and then proceed to fuck me, moving your fingers magically inside me. I'm groaning yes, open me, take me. I'm in my body completely, my cunt is me, I'm lost, it's heaven, it's beyond that, I'm flying in space where I want to be.

Keeping your fingers in me, you undo the belt round my wrists, and help me to roll over on my back. I want more, are you going to stop? You massage my wrists and then stretch each arm out and up. Carefully the cuffs are strapped on and each wrist is chained to the corner of the bed. Then deliberately, you attend to my ankles. I'm on my back, my legs wide open, body stretched, breasts, belly, cunt, my centre. Now looking at me, reaching up and rolling my nipples one after the other, you let yourself go, fucking me leisurely at first, and then harder and harder, telling me to open more, open all the way, and I do, I do, I do, until I feel such a bearing down from my womb, such a concentration of sensation flowing from my cunt, from my clit, up up and around my whole body, into my head, that I think I'll explode.

I'm making noises I have no choice about.

The upside of my cunt is going to explode, a different kind of coming. A surge and a levelling, my cunt is still open, but soft and satisfied, you breath deeply and move out. There is a sweetness between us now as you kneel between my legs, then lower to reach me with your mouth. Then you lick and suck me to bliss, until my cries match the magic of my orgasm and I come and come and you stay with me, keeping the wave going, riding along with it; keep it going honey, yes. Then your fingers, still in me, but quiet, move again, and as I glide down you meet my cunt and I cry out as I feel an after image of the orgasm.

You unloosen the ties from my wrists and I reach up to you and draw you down onto me and hold you, calming, savouring, and finally laughing, exhausted from it all.

◆ ◆ ◆

Hey lover, I've got incredibly hot imagining all this, I've been moving around like a demon on my chair as I type madly. I want you to emerge from the screen feet first, legs apart. Kissing it is not enough. I want to move onto your cunt fast and furious, move into you rough and ready, right now. Get your ass through that screen girl!

SEX AND WATER

SARAH KAY

It was the third day of Chanukah. I know because I had just scraped the wax out of the tiny candle holders on Ella's menorah. Such behaviour was not usual. Normally, on getting up, the last thing I do is to go and clean the utensils of the night before. But I was still trying to impress Ella, my girlfriend from Chicago. In any event, I had gone down to make coffee — a notion more romantic in suggestion than reality — coffee always makes me run to the toilet. First, my stomach starts to creak and then the lining separates itself from the walls, like old paint peeling off ... but enough already! What I really planned to write about isn't coffee at all, nor is it Chanukah, nor, for that matter, is it toilets. What I thought I'd tell you about, however, is sex — sex in the bath.

Actually it is relevant that it was the day of the third night. For being Chanukah it was cold, very cold. My toes hardened like Shabbat bread crusts as I crept downstairs, and I could feel my nipples sharpening in the gusts of air as I approached and drew past the front door. Since Ella's arrival we had stopped wearing night clothes. Having transcended geographical distance, we rebuffed any possible separation caused by cloth, buttons and zippers. So at night, lying in bed, we shivered together, holding on tight, parting only to rush to the bathroom and back. Sometimes at a speed owing more to modesty than cold: my brother was around at the time too. Since his return we each had experienced the discomfort of being trapped in the bathroom, rendered immobile by his presence on the stairs. Forced to sit — cold buttocks on hard plastic — until the click of his bedroom door allowed us to make an escape.

Maybe then it was the cold and the failure of coffee to warm. Or perhaps it was that sense of festivity and indulgence which always accompanies Chanukah. Or perhaps it was neither. But I found myself at three pm (waiting for Ella who was removing a tampon in the toilet opposite) in the bathroom, with its rose coloured tiles, stained bath and steamed mirror. There's not much else to say — a very average bathroom — though perhaps I could just mention the pre-chrome taps and the broken shower head spurting water everywhere. This may or may not be relevant.

So as I brushed my teeth, examining with mounting anxiety the pimples above my breasts, Ella entered. She looked, as she always does, gorgeous. Broad hips, round stomach, full breasts. Sand coloured hair kissing the tops of her thighs. She smiled, leaning on one foot and asked,

'Is the water hot?'

Our conversations in the bathroom always tended towards a degree of repetition, unnoticeable elsewhere.

'Yeah, seems okay. Though I think we're the last, so goodness knows how long it will stay that way.'

Ella bent over over the tub and ran fingers smelling of musk and sex under the tap. They reddened as our scent carried upwards in the heat, filling the small room with its sweet pungency. Caught in a wave of lust and longing, I clambered quickly and gracelessly into the bath. Ella, more tentative, followed, letting her body slowly sink beneath the surface. I watched as her breasts rose to float weightlessly on the rising water. Ella's eyes were closed. Her face was glistening from the steam. From my position near the taps, I bent over and kissed her eyelids, trailing my fingers through the water above her torso. The currents tickled her skin. She smiled, but her eyes stayed closed.

Outside it was already dusk. Occasional cars shot round the corner, streaking the walls with yellow light. Their reflection danced on my body, caught between Ella's legs. Experimenting in the months since her arrival, we had discovered that this was the most efficient way to share a bath. And sometimes, when the urge outweighed the hurry, I would lie back on her body, a thin film of water between us, while she soaped my arms, breasts and anything else within reach.

Now sitting in the bath, with Ella's legs on either side, my palms travelling down have reached that place where surfaces become spaces, skin — hair, and what was convex — concave.

Hesitantly I moved my hand between her thighs to stroke the curls of hair, parting the tangles to touch lips that shyly protrude. Caressing them with the tips of my fingers, I slowly began to nudge the warm skin open. It yielded and I entered, into warmth and darkness, pulsating with the murmurs of pleasure and life. Ella watched me — self-conscious, aroused — as I stroked and teased each lip, feeling it contract and close behind me. Her intake of breath sharpened as I entered and filled the darkness at the base of her clitoris. At first, from this angle, my fingers could not find her opening. Gently I probed until the flesh slid apart, taking me up and in, to caress new textures and surfaces.

Then, like a soul who has discovered dovening after a lifetime of contemplation, Ella began to move. The rhythm of our breathing matched the motion of her body. Lifting wide hips to encompass me better, she swiftly let go, leaving my dislodged fingers entangled in the surrounding curls. I returned to her lips. This time the pressure of my body was behind the movement of my wrist against her thighs. Her lips and clitoris were becoming darker, thickening with my touch, as blood filled the tissues. Ella shivered, the water was getting cold. There was no heat this late in the afternoon and I could feel the drafts. After all, it was the third day of Chanukah.

I let the hot water surge into the bath, ignoring tell-tale drips on the carpet. If it soaked through, someone would come to complain, but until then .... With growing recklessness I stretched out fully along Ella's body, involuntarily moaning with pleasure as our mouths and tongues touched — sounds of desire hidden in the rushing water. Below, distorted in the swirling motion, Ella's nipples formed a unique maze of ridges and valleys rising to two soft plateaus. Without thinking I lowered my head to engulf a breast, but rose immediately, choking. Threads of water streamed out of both nostrils, leaving a trail of bubbles that lay momentarily on the wet skin below. But as yet I was undeterred. With a gulp of steamy air, I returned — diving down beneath the water's surface to envelope a soft nipple in my mouth. Licking at its base, it grew hard against my tongue, a breast clenched, hot and wet, between my teeth.

Then suddenly we were moving harder and faster and louder, struggling in the enclosed space to stretch and pull. I pushed down and Ella shouted. Water surged over the edge, drowning the mat, seeping down through to the pale green carpet.

'Sar, phone!'

The voice filled my head with visions of wet towels and cold, dripping bodies. Why the fuck must it be now? And how long had he been standing there?

'Who is it?' I yelled back, fuelled by the energy of an orgasm lost forever.

'Dunno. Sounds like a meeting.'

'Shit! I'm in the bath. Tell them to ring back in half an hour.'

'How come you're still in the bath?'

'Oh go away,' I whispered into Ella's breasts and stomach, tracing the curves with my fingers and memory.

But Ella had had enough. Smothering her laughter, she pushed me up until we were both sitting cross-legged, a shampoo bottle and bar of soap between us,

'Next time, my turn. Okay?' she said.

I WATCH AS YOU UNDRESS

JULIE A BENNETT

I watch as you undress
never tiring of your curves
I feel a dampness between my legs
my heart pounds for release
How I ache to feel your lips on mine
Impatient for your power
Rise to your role in our games.

Push me down onto our bed
Slowly release all of my buttons
Slip your finger into my cunt
Watch my nipples grow into anticipation
make me cry out for that sweet release.

Tie my hands bind me strong
Make me want you more
I feel your tongue on my lips
The force of your body pressing into mine
Knowing it's only a game
no power needed
only a game
Force my legs open

REMEMBRANCE SUNDAY

DAISY KEMPE

She would rather have taken her photograph.

Several photographs. A ten by eight portrait. A series of portraits. Some in repose. A few shivering on the brink of movement. Catching the steady clear gaze of Beatrice's eyes. Far too clear. Daisy's own vision unsteady as she remembered the penetrating blue of the eyes. Was it the same shade as the shirt? Cornflower blue and white convict stripes. Neat evenly spaced stripes. Nothing flamboyant about Beatrice Lane's appearance. The top button, no, the top two buttons, undone. The third button curving gently over the small breasts. Daisy Kingdom did not feel gentle remembering. She had no great wish to remember. She would rather take photographs.

Black and white of course would not do. Blue comes out black. It was all coming out black. Memory, she realized with frustration, pays little attention to our wishes. Remembrance is defiantly colour blind.

Daisy was waiting for Benn and with a certain amount of anger, was remembering Beatrice. Memory seemed to be the one feature in her disciplined lifestyle she could not control. Benn, she found easier to control, perhaps because, at twenty-eight, the young bookshop owner was the same age as Daisy's tempestuous son Dan and Beatrice's son Charlie, the one with his mother's keen blue eyes and stubborn character.

Daisy had exactly an hour before Benn Quirk closed up the family bookshop, inevitably named Quirks, drove to the country and attempted to disturb her. There was no time for memories, no time for feelings that after all these months, she still could not handle.

In her white walled room, dressed predictably from head to foot in white ... even her red brown plait braided with white ribbon ... Daisy pitted her considerable will against a series of memories, which perched like malignant crows on the rims of the chalky leather armchairs. Today's newly purchased seats, like yesterday's hard purchased self, had been taken over by evocations of Beatrice Lane. The woman, it seemed, still possessed an unsurpassed quality for ownership and control.

Daisy, annoyed, pulled at her plait. Neither she nor her new house would brook repossession. She had changed the lenses. She had refocussed her attention on her work. And at weekends on Benn. Young Benn was what the quiet bookseller was usually called, as distinct from Old Ben, the famous father, head of the family business, who had made his name and increased his capital as best selling crime writer Benjamin B Quirk.

Young Benn had been good to Daisy these last hard months, easing her inflexible work routine, encouraging her to have some fun. Daisy doubted if she could have got through the difficult days without Benn's constancy. Momentarily she felt hemmed in by the recognition and tugged furiously at her hair. Some straggling chestnut brown strands had escaped from the severity of the braid. More brown than chestnut these days but at least the grey was well covered. Her hair was the one item in her territory Daisy did not want to see white. At fifty-six, she was as vain as Beatrice had accused her of being at thirty-six during their first heated encounter, in Beatrice's blazing brown and orange sitting room. An occasion of furious argument, every syllable of which Daisy had meticulously recorded on tape.

For a second her eyes flickered indulgently to the Tandberg Audio Tutor 771. The faded black print on the front of the taperecorder stated: "Educational with Dynamic Sound." Yes, it had certainly been that. She grinned, thinking about it. Automatically her mind switched down the play button. Suddenly Daisy's clinical white workplace, whose only consistent noise was the cold clatter of metallic machinery, was filled with red hot sounds from the past.

Anger. Arguments. Jokes and joy. A wild hilarity, and sometimes weariness as the children squabbled. Teatime tantrums. The constant whirr of the tapes. Always the same sounds. Then, by ten pm .... Dan and Charlie upstairs with their homework, little Suzie at last in bed .... passion and peace. Uncertain certitudes, scheduled to last for centuries.

But they had not.

Perhaps colour prints were the answer. Beatrice in some moods was too vivid, too unpredictable, for black and white, although they grappled with her strength well enough. Colour photographs would be more appropriate to catch Beatrice Lane's ash blonde hair, streaked with bands of grey; yes, colour would do credit to the blue and white striped convict shirt, and to the soft blue velvet jacket. The tailored severe surface that hid the tensions within. Nothing could do credit to the softness of that jacket. Nothing could do credit to the softness of that skin. How many months had it been, after their first meeting, before Daisy had touched the azure blue of that jacket pulled up high across the shirt, open just slightly at the neck?

Daisy looked out of the window. No houses opposite. Crumpled green woodland for miles. Scratchy brown bark, a few leaves falling onto the window pane. Chosen for the endless unpeopled space. Privacy at last. Green ... everywhere was green. Calm and dull like the walls of the hospital ward she had spent many weeks in after the news. Not that the news had had anything to do with her accident. She had always driven the white sports car too fast. Had always been prone to accidents. Now she lived safely, had sold the car, cycled a lot, lived in the country, surrounded by plenty of solid safe green. She took occasional visits to the sea with Benn, being careful never to visit Cornwall, where every view remorselessly reminded her of the times with Beatrice and the children.

She remembered how Suzie, the youngest, had bubbled with excitement over the pleasures of the small fishing village. Some evenings it had strained their patience trying to persuade the child to get off to bed.

'What's the point?' Suzie had said to Beatrice. 'Nothing special ever happens after I go. You two only do dull things.'

Nothing special, thought Daisy. Just being together by the sea. Today she was glad she did not look out on the sea. The sea was the wrong colour. That was the problem with the sea. Blue like the eyes, like the shirt, like the jacket that buttoned her mind back into the past. Why had Beatrice never taken off that damn jacket? Eighty-two degrees outside the conference room, their first meeting place, all the other women stripping off, and Beatrice Lane, who had carefully described herself as a staid librarian, calmly buttoned up her striped shirt, and hugged the hot velvet jacket more closely about her shoulders.

Daisy looked down at her hands. Short working fingers which not even memory had removed from the typewriter keys. She gave a wry smile. She was after all only an amateur photographer. By trade, if that is what it was, Daisy was a professional writer. Not, she thought grimly, quite as professional as Old Ben Quirk, whose successful pile of glossy hardbacks were lavishly displayed near the Quirks' cash till. A winning situation. At the side of the shop Benn had carefully mounted Daisy's small select number of paperbacks. No, she was certainly no amateur.

Amateurs play around with people's faces. Bits of scenery. Enlarge and diminish landscapes. Move the trees, or the truth, about a bit. Furniture amongst a green wilderness. Professionals do something similar, but they don't play around.

I broke you, she thought pedantically, passion put aside as she carefully typed the words: I BROKE YOU. I stopped you smiling. I stopped that terrifying calm. For a moment, you stopped looking serene and beautiful. What we had was savage. In the mornings we faced the neighbours like middle-aged good companions, hoping they hadn't identified last night's noises, and talked about the boys' progress at the village comprehensive. Then at night we touched and tore at each other's flesh and brought each other to the point where peeing and crying was the only relief from so much held in passion. I do not know how to record that with a camera. Difficult being an amateur. Limited skills.

In the early days of the decade with Beatrice, her skills had been used for research. Questioning, recording, capturing in sound, pinning down in words, tiny fragments of truth which could be collected, collated, refurbished and framed. 'Careful you don't set us in amber,' Beatrice had warned one day, giving her a hug. Easy to see why Daisy had later turned to photography.

She had recorded everything. The lines and the lies. The struggle to survive. The problems with the boys. The hostility of their fathers. The fears of the custody cases. The faithfulness of their friends. The laughs, most of all the laughs. But never the passion, never the power. Never the Sundays when the children were usually away with their fathers or grandparents.

Daisy glanced down at her wristwatch. Silver, significant and expensive, on a cheap white leather strap. Benn had given it to her for her last birthday. Originally it had possessed a matching silver wristband. Daisy had changed it. There were days when she felt irrationally controlled by Benn's warmth and generosity.

Occasionally she made impetuous silly stands, hurting Benn, then deeply regretting it. She still wanted to punish her lover for things that were not Benn's fault. Just like Old Ben had.

Beatrice had sent her a simple birthday card with a photo of the sea. Inside, she had written 'Love Bea' and the date. Nothing else. For nine and a half years they had continued to send each other cards for birthdays and at Christmas, and from any exotic holidays which they had taken separately. It was called keeping in touch. The last postcard from Beatrice had come a few weeks after the birthday card. Six months ago. It was from Thailand. Then silence. There had been no further postcards. No more could be expected. Communication had closed down. In another month Daisy knew she would face the first Christmas without a card.

The watch, which recorded days as well as time, informed her it was six o'clock Saturday evening. Benn was due to arrive from the bookshop in a little over an hour for what was left of the weekend. Daisy still had a batch of photos to process, another chapter to finish. For a few minutes she felt under seige, then she thought about Benn and relaxed. If she was still writing she could trust Benn to understand. Considerate and caring about her work, her lover was an excellent cook who had developed expert nurturing skills from years of practice in the Quirk household where everyone paid constant attention to Old Ben's autocratic whims. This year at least Benn took quiet care of the Sundays.

In view of the lateness of the hour, it would be foolish to remember those other Sundays. Benn more than anyone deserved her full attention for at least one day a week. Daisy could not afford to waste any more time. She flicked open her work, then shut it again. She put a clean sheet of paper into the typewriter, took it out, tore it up. You can't tear up memories. Foolish or not, Daisy could not forget that last Sunday, despite the fact that it was ten years ago. No, not quite. It was nine years, eleven months, three weeks, and six days ago.

That particular Sunday morning was with her now.

Beatrice was huddled in their low brown bed. Sobbing and struggling with the truth she despaired facing and the risks she feared taking against the cosy life she had built up, and the pretences she leant on to give her stability in a profession that offered her little if the reality of her life with Daisy was exposed. Beatrice's shoulders shuddered. Her cries were like wails. Her eyes. Daisy had not wanted to look into her eyes. Such wildness should be private. Daisy distanced from the distress, had lain still on the bed, waiting for the storm to subside, waiting for Beatrice to talk. She felt chilled, already prepared.

'There were so many times I wished you'd go away. Or wished the book would go away. Even though I needed you here, wanted you here. But you never did,' Beatrice said still sobbing.

Daisy remembered saying 'No I never did.' That was all she could remember saying, though she suspected she had said a lot more at the time.

'I've lived with what you have been doing, what we have been doing for years. I've lived with the tapes, with the words, I've believed in it like you have. I still do. I was almost sorry when the white light got switched off and I was no longer part of the process. When you shut yourself away, spent all your time working, when all we had was the structure, us as a household, the children, it was like you had stopped paying me any real attention.'

Beatrice was crying again. Quite out of control with crying. She would remember that later. She would despise that later. Daisy had denied some of it but she had felt helpless, alienated, not wanting to understand. She had got out of the bed, gone to the bathroom, and brought back two blue loo rolls. 'Try these love, maybe you can get through both of them.' They had laughed, and held each other. Daisy had thought of platitudes. We'll win through. We'll try again. We love each other. She had tried them all out in her head. Rejected them all. Had said nothing. She already knew what decisions Beatrice had come to.

Slowly Beatrice spoke again, her words now muffled by a pillow. 'Our life has been filled with words, and sounds, but there are words we can't seem to say. We probably shan't be able to say them for a long time.' Then she stopped crying and still hanging on to Daisy she said, 'You know that I've met somebody else. I know what you think, you think it's absurd. It may turn out not to be important, not in the long run, but at this moment it is important for me to go ahead. I have to do that.'

Did Daisy say unfairly: 'You'll do what you want. You always do what you want,' believing it fair at the time? Or did she merely think it? Hurting someone you care about is always fair if you feel hurt yourself. What she did remember saying, apparently unruffled, surprised at how restrained she sounded: 'You'll go away for a bit?'

'Oh yes, I'll probably go away for a bit,' Beatrice had answered, calm in her turn. 'It's what people do, isn't it?' They had both laughed, as if the very suggestion was idiotic, belonged to two other people.

I didn't really want to drive you out, one of them had murmured. Or perhaps they had not. Not then. Not on that particular Sunday. Perhaps that was something one of them had said later. If they had said it at all. 'I do love you, you know that.' Certainly one of them had said that, or maybe both, said it again and again, like a mantra, an incantation, a protective blanket of words against the horrors to come. Love anyway had in the end very little to do with it. They had gone on loving each other but each small action they took from that Sunday onwards altered the course of the rest of their lives, as those kind of minor alterations do.

Daisy, skilled at recalling acceptable versions, juggled in her mind several accounts of the words they had spoken, then decided she really did not remember what exactly had been said. Ten years had given her time enough to rewrite them all. What did remain clear, as clear and as striking as the events of the previous Sunday spent with Benn on a local beach, was not the words at all.

She remembered Beatrice's lips brushing hers, she remembered watching Beatrice's face lift, her lips coming full down covering her own. She took them gently down to Daisy's breast. Daisy's nipples were ready for her mouth. Daisy exhuded the emotion and heat she had been stifling in her chilled body for days, as she and Beatrice had prepared for a cold hard Sunday. Beatrice became more passionate than Daisy could ever recall her being. Ironic in the circumstances. While they made love, or perhaps it was just before they were fully folded, Beatrice had whispered: 'I'm scared Daisy.' It must have been before, they had never had those kind of conversations during.

Strange Daisy thought, how with men, fucking with men, she had always needed to talk before, after and particularly during. Their bodies were never enough. She had always needed their words to help her connect. Usually their words were not the right ones, and she wished she had written the script herself. To her surprise she did not talk much with Benn either. Words were inessential, it was Benn's presence which composed her. Sometimes the strong touch drove out the thoughts of Beatrice. Her new lover was not touching her now, but was marking up books, being helpful to customers, getting ready for the long drive. For the next hour there was no bulwark against the imminent haunting.

Daisy's hands roved across Beatrice's thighs. She had pulled the duvet back. It was a November morning, but still warm, and she wanted to see Beatrice's hairs. She was always intrigued by their darkness. Everything else about her was fair.

'Did you know the hairs on the cunt never go grey?' Beatrice had said sleepily. Her cunt was very large compared with the rest of her body. Her shoulders were slim, her tummy flat, her breasts small. Daisy would tease her about them. 'Two little white boobs.'

Beatrice, grumpy, would retort: 'They work all right. Look at the kids.'

Yet she had been self-conscious about their size and Daisy had never understood why. Beatrice's small white breasts made her hold her breath as she thought about sucking them. Her small white breasts and her darker cunt. She wanted to trail her fingers through its darkness. Wanted to push hard into its deepness. Push until it hurt. To feel it wet. Feel it hard and wet first before it moved and melted on her pushing finger. It was the second before her hand touched Beatrice. That second was the one she always feared, was always trembling for. It was the guide to her mind, to their minds. Would she part for her finger?

'My palm runneth over,' Beatrice once said with delight when she came upon Daisy fast. 'I love you dripping all down my hand.' Daisy's own hand hurried. Then she stayed it a moment. 'Rest a minute,' Beatrice had said. Daisy paused. They had time now. Did they? How much time did they have? They had all the time in the world because limits had suddenly been set on it.

'Why are you scared?' Daisy had asked. 'No need to be.' She was scared herself, scared but excited. Beatrice was murmuring: 'You are scary, you won't let me retreat.' 'No I won't.' Daisy was relieved that Beatrice knew. Terrible things were about to overtake them and she felt secure lying there beside Beatrice. Content. Even safe. She did not usually have time to work out what she felt. Not when they were loving. There wasn't usually time for dissection. Bodies fly too fast. Minds tip over bodies' edges. That Sunday was more gradual. They were both planning it out delicately. They both wanted it to be right. They both wanted to let go yet keep in each other's hold. Be able to recall some of it later. That loving was crucial Daisy had thought at the time and certainly later.

She had come first willingly, slowly, moving as Beatrice's hands guided. She was able to keep herself above the battles of her own body. She concentrated on making Beatrice come. She willed her to come loudly. Yes, my quiet blue librarian love, I wanted you loud and long. And you came that way. Very loud for a very long time. Beatrice Lane, severe blue librarian, was actually screaming. Beatrice Lane, no longer in the tailored blue jacket, was screaming and crying louder than the loudest boy leaving the quiet library. Beatrice Lane, screamed and raved and spilt herself shuddering as Daisy's fingers, then her hand pressed in further and further. Her hand was streaming with Beatrice's wetness, the bed was pungent with Beatrice's smell, the room in shock from Beatrice's screams. Thank goodness it was Sunday and the children were away.

Daisy's hand was soaked, the bed was suddenly soaked too, she wanted to taste her wetness, taste it everywhere. There was no time for her to shift positions. Beatrice was making her come with her as she came again. Another sheet would have to hit the washing machine later, Daisy thought triumphantly. Her screams are mine. Mine are hers. I hear them. They fade. No thoughts. Feel, just feel. They were both smiling. Both sweating with desire, the stained sheet, hot and crumpled, beneath them. One of them had said, 'Do the neighbours ever notice and wonder at our persistent cleanliness with our one Habitat brown sheet? Maybe we should buy a second.' Did the thought occur that they might not ever again need a second sheet? Probably not, they had stopped thinking.

Drift with it. Fly with it. Fall into it. Steady. Don't let go of her. Keep your hand steady so she turns on your hand. Thrusts against it. Away from it. Magnetic. She *has* to twist back on it. It dissolves. I dissolve. I feel what I do to her in my cunt. Impossible. Is it her body or mine? It does not matter. It feels right. In my head. Lock. Twist. Turn. Key. Fit. Bone. Press bone. It slides. We slide.

No one else in the whole damn judgemental world ever makes me feel this way.

Yes that was how it was Daisy thought, gripping hard on to the typewriter keys, her eyes filling with tears. No one else.

Go back. Feel that way back. Go back in. Back and in. I slip in again, deep into her and move for her to thrust into me. My clitoris and hers circle on hands. Arch on finger tips. Head circles. Her clit is mine. I breathe 'My clit. My clit. Come ON. Come ON'. A hand is over my mouth. I want to lie back and be suffocated. I am helpless and powerful. She hears. Her pink moistness showing through black hairs responds. She makes sounds. Tongues. Then words. 'I want to FUCK you'. Violence beneath the joy. Joy in the violence. Shut ears to sounds. My sounds. Her sounds. Keep moving. Know what I do even as I begin again. Edge in sight but too pleasurable, too painful, to let myself be swept over. Stop. Don't stop. Stop. Don't stop. Screw me. Screw me. I say it to her. She loves it, eats it up. No stopping now. You great fuck. You great, great fuck. Strange to hurl into our rushing, to toss savagely within it, yet to be above the tossing. Inside. Outside. Both bodies alarmed, exhausted, by clever planning fingers which know exactly the spots, never miss the points for pleasure.

Difficult to write this without recalling and wanting her here now. Wanting to splatter her cool blue beauty with red and orange heat right across my neat white carpeted floor. Want her down, want her down on that floor, on a Saturday night, with the sounds of all the machines in the world screaming like her screams in my ice white workroom, only minutes before Benn's arrival. Just like that night aeons ago when they had made furious love on the old brown and white carpet recovering themselves only minutes before Charlie and Dan's arrival back from their father's.

The boys. The boys and Benn. Grown men all three of them. Even Suzie, the youngest, had slid into a well paid media job and seldom visited. Daisy took a deep breath, pulled herself back from the past, and thought about those she still cared for. Neither Dan nor Charlie took her relationship with Benedict Quirk seriously though they had nothing against him. Charlie in fact had met Benn at college, had once been quite friendly with him. Today Charlie was dully indifferent to everything to do with Daisy and Benn, resenting them both.

Dan, her son, a sensitive young man, and Suzie, a fierce young feminist, with an acute grasp on the new ideology would not think well of Daisy's immersion into lust. Past or present. It was lesbian erotica or spiritual engagement nowadays and the words had moved on, matched up. But there you have it kids, Daisy said to herself, smiling. Twenty years ago, when we first met, it was fucking and screwing and when we did it at forty I hope, Dan and Charlie, as children of twelve you and Benn were getting yourselves a good education. Beatrice and I were. Education with Dynamic Sound! She slid her hand round the smooth loved body of the tape recorder that had played such an integral part in those years. Holding on to the machine her mind slipped away from Benedict, the boys and Suzie, and back to that Sunday.

Daisy had wanted her on any floor, in any field, in any bed, particularly a bed that wasn't theirs, (had they tried a children's bunk, or was that just one of their jokes?) in railway carriages, on buses, dangerously, ecstatically, in cars driven too fast. Often across the breakfast table, remembering last night, or at the tea table speculating silently about the next night. Each of them had been able to rip each others clothes off with just their eyes meeting across the table. As the children ate fish fingers and mash, they drank a slow glass of red wine and made each other wet and fierce as they gazed steadily across at each other.

'Sometimes Bea, you look at Mummy real funny, in a funny way,' Suzie had once said perceptively. 'What are you trying to tell Mummy that you don't want us to know?' The elder boys laughed.

Suzie was known for her curiosity. Did the boys know? Did they know that Daisy wanted her anywhere. Everywhere. Everytime. From the first day at that Conference. Was that why the last Sunday was no cooler or stranger than those that had come before? Passion was never the problem, any more than love was.

They had made love for hours. Sometimes one of them resisting, sometimes the other. What Daisy remembered, gloated over even, was when Beatrice suddenly stopped resisting. Gave in quite suddenly. Shouting the words that turned them both on. Daisy knew she would have come sooner, more steadily, if she had gone into her vagina. That was the easy way. But she did not. Beatrice came the hard way. Sweating. She rarely sweated. Face twisting. Beautiful face not beautiful now. Real face. Real force. In everything that mattered Beatrice could be trusted to come the hard way, the necessary way, despite her love of ease and comfort. That was what Daisy admired most about her.

It was later. 'That was extraordinary,' Beatrice had said. Eyes shining. A quizzical grin at the edges of her mouth. She was almost back to looking beautiful and cool. She had been ugly with our fierceness when she came. Not often I see her like that. Glad to have seen her like that. Strong and unprotected. A different kind of beauty. No mask. Passion with her contorts, not distorts. She is encircled with disguises. Onion rings of pretence. Perhaps her cool beauty is another screen. To look as she looks most days, the days she gets lustful looks from other people, you have to appear serene, disinterested. You have to challenge people to wreck you with loving. The calm is only her surface.

The day before that particular Sunday, preparing for a science project in the library, she had told Daisy about surface tensions. Demonstrated how to break them. It made loving that Sunday memorable. First her tension, hatred, resentment, then tearing apart in hysteria. Frightened. Small. Then opening wide in desire. Lusting for it. Followed by enormous tenderness, then peace.

Daisy's fear of destruction over. Hers too. A temporary closeness. Already Daisy was listening to the words just out of hearing. Already she was charting the changes in their life. Mapping out responses. Hardening herself. She lay next to Beatrice and knew then they would come, there would be small alteration after small alteration, compromising their life together. But for the moment they lay motionless. Beatrice looked tranquil, and because of that she looked like her photos.

On consideration, black and white *were* always the best. Beatrice liked them the best. She always said her beauty was a trial, an impediment. But the day they had their passport photos taken in the Post Office photo booth, and hers came out ugly she snatched them out of Daisy's hand and tore them up.

When Beatrice had flown to Thailand, had she still been vain? Had she still been a woman cool on the outside and raw and immoderate within? The postcards from exotic places don't tell you those facts. Not even that last one, the one from Thailand, had given Daisy much insight. It was a photo of the complex canal system in Bangkok where the markets front the water's edge. People were scurrying through the markets, looking busy and happy. Had Beatrice been amongst them? Had she been happy? The card offered Daisy no clues. She would have to rely on her memories.

Photographers can hint at the truth, if the sitter allows. Writers can play around with ideas that suggest it. But, Daisy sharply reminded herself, professionals are not supposed to play around. Professionals mean business. Writing was her business. The way she paid her mortgage on the new white house. The house with no room for blue memories, the house with no brown or orange cushions, no brown or orange blazing bedsitting room; the neutral toned writer's residence where with cold calculation a fifty-six year old professional woman earned a reasonable living. Waited reasonably, between chapters, for her twenty-eight year old lover. There was no longer anything unreasonable in Daisy's narrow life.

Nearly ten years of living without Beatrice, living alone, struggling with the words, had finally seen to that.

To write now about Beatrice she would have to take it seriously. Obtain a large advance. Make some royalties from it.

She would rather have taken her photograph.

She looked again at her watch, then at the large calendar on the white wall. Tomorrow was Remembrance Sunday. It was a good time to commemorate the dead. For a second, she shrank back from the sound of the word.

Dead. In the six months since the news of the plane crash she had not been able to use it. A cold November Saturday night was a reasonable time to start. She began to type fast and efficiently.

Benn would be there to take care of Sunday.

He had been caretaking for some time now. Five weeks after the news had been broken to Daisy, Benn had come to visit her. He had brought her some of Beatrice's possessions. Letters and tapes, several albums of photos. It was the first time she had met him. He was still bandaged, still badly scarred. But as he said, lucky to be alive. He was one of the only three survivors of the crash.

That is if you did not count Daisy.

NEAT AS AN OYSTER

BERTA R FREISTADT

Neat as an oyster
She lay on my bed
My mouth watered

Her face
Is the sweet moon
I watch by
Sleepless till dawn

Both gnats and I
Bite her
On her softest skin
But more considerate
I leave no marks
And so
She lets me in

Outside her window
The trees
Are a waterfall
Of birdsong

IT'S OLLIE YOU CRUISED AT THE DOCTORS

JO FISK

I am very nervous. Today I hear whether I got the job. Two hours from now I'll pick up the telephone. I am exhausted too. Last night I went to a Brixton club and spent the night gazing at a clique of muscly dykes flexing their arms and stroking each other with an eye on the crowd below.

I am in my doctor's waiting room reading August's *Vogue*. It's ten thirty and my parking meter runs out at ten forty. The receptionist wears a watch pinned to her chest and she terrifies me. However, I am freshly-bathed and look it, with a faint sweat just above my mouth.

'Excuse me. How long will it be now?' The receptionist turns to me.

'You're number six. The doctor's on number four now.'

As I turn to pick up my briefcase from the orange plastic chair, my attention is arrested by a leather jacket. A dyke? Spiky black hair and blue eyes. She could be. I fix on her eyes. Why doesn't she look at me?

Back on my chair I root around the bottom of my briefcase for twenty pence bits. Two are not enough. In exasperation I look around. She is approaching my side of the room. Excitement overrides parking-meter anxiety. She walks with a don't-mess-with-me air, heavy boots moving fast with a surprising lack of clumsy noise.

I cannot believe it when she sits in the next chair. She ignores me but I cannot take my eyes off her. Open lips, chin thrust forward, sunken cheeks with the remnants of almost lost dimples. Her fists are clenched and she keeps shifting one boot on top of the other. I have a sense of precariously held in energy. Was she also awake all night, but too hyped up to relax next day?

'Where did you get your jacket?' I ask casually. She turns her head and looks at me.

'Kensington Market. Do you want to try it on?'

'Yeah. Why not?' Hiding my surprise at her offer.

We stand up and take our jackets off. I cannot look at her.

It fits me snugly, moulding to my body like a lover.

'I like this.'

'It looks good.'

In the course of the next five minutes we discover those important details about city of origin, response to London, source of income or lack thereof. I can hardly concentrate. This is one gorgeous patient.

'Have you got any twenty pence bits?'

'I hardly know you and you're extorting money from me.'

I look in her eyes and find myself moving towards her like a drunk about to headbutt the pavement. I have to get out of here. I am hot.

'If the doctor calls my name say I'm feeding the meter. I'll be back in five minutes.' I stand ready to stride off, neck burning.

A hand grips my arm.

'What's your name?' She forces me down on the chair again.

'Jude Henry. What's yours?'

'Ollie. Would you like to meet tonight? I have to go to work after the doctor.'

We arrange to meet. She doesn't show. She calls me at work and I'm out on some worthless expedition. She has no telephone. I am frustrated and bore my colleagues to death with my obsession. I got the job I applied for but have to work out one month's notice where I am. I cannot settle down at work. My feet will not keep still. Every time the telephone goes my nervousness shoots to my mouth and hands. I decide to blank her image from my mind.

A week later, the telephone:

'It's Ollie you cruised at the doctors.'

Dejected in anticipation of being stood up I order coffee in the late night Soho cafe we arranged to meet in and find a table without even one neurotic glimpse at the mirror tiles. I look at an abandoned *Evening Standard*, yawning glumly.

Something touches my neck and I jump. Ollie is at the next table. She had been there watching me as I made my myopic entrance and sat down without spotting her. Could that look good?

Ollie has lost a tooth. She had it smashed out by a man who attacked her.

'At least he didn't rape me. I've been raped four times. I have to recover my confidence now. It's hard. I was assaulted as a child too — or should one refer to it as abuse? I have to stop identifying as victim.'

'So do I. So do I.' I'm back to being twelve in my head, the pain and confusion of adult male fingers probing inside, squeezing child nipples. It has thrown me, this strong-looking black-clad dyke instantly sensing my history and confiding her own. We talk without fear of silent recrimination from those who would rather not hear.

I get more coffee. Her eyes are unashamedly on my thighs as I walk back. My tight black 501s move on my skin as I walk. I imagine it's her hands. She has to know how I want her. The flushed neck is a dead giveaway.

'So what were you doing at the doctors that day?' Ollie asks as I put the coffee down. 'You look healthy enough.'

'I have herpes. I had to get some ointment.'

'I have it too. Did you get it off a bloke?'

'Yeah.'

We nod disgruntedly at each other.

'I went to get something off the doctor for my tummy. It's stress. Work. You know.'

'I do.'

'She was brilliant. She gave me a note off work for the week.'

Ollie has tickets for a mixed gay north London club. We leave the coffee scented warmth and face the November iciness.

'So who do you live with?' Sus out any competition.

'Becky. She makes videos. Last week she did one of me using a huge Japanese state-of-the-art vibrator with all sorts of amazing attachments.'

'I'd like to see it sometime,' I murmur coolly.

'I'd like to watch you.'

Our breath freezes in the air. Ollie grinds her jaws in futile defence against the weather. I look at a group of trendy straights huddled outside a club in Wardour Street. A thuggish looking lad behind them shouts, 'Queer cunts!' Fear snakes its way up the inside of my legs. Automatically I move away from Ollie and we quicken our stride, remaining at opposite sides of the pavement and ignoring each other.

In my icy heaterless car Ollie rests her arm along the back of the driving seat and runs her fingertips over my ears. I am acutely conscious of all the space around my body, all the bits she isn't touching: the neglected limbs and aching core of me now sensitized by Ollie's attention and fingers.

At the club I order my first and last whisky of the evening. I remember a time when I had to be virtually unconscious in order to go to bed with another person.

'So what turns you on?' Ollie demands.

'My fantasies are totally right-off. Tell me yours instead.'

'I have one about being fourteen in bed with another girl. Some street-wise older woman character — say, forty, same age as me now — finds us, watches us writhing against each other until we're exhausted, drags us out of bed, stings our faces with her hand and fucks us in turn while the other watches, frustrated.'

'I like it.'

Ollie rubs my knee in thanks. My legs open, one falling against her tensed thigh.

Ollie cannot refuse me tonight after that disclosure. Surely not? Or does she get off on making a woman need her badly and then walking away?

Ollie demands a taste of my perverted fantasy catalogue. I'm freaked out and vulnerable:

'They're gross. Adult men fucking children of both sexes. Me being him. Me punching my ex-lover out and attacking her. Violent rape. You name it. If it's gross I have it.'

I am angry, but not with Ollie. Ollie is silent gazing at me with water threatening to flood out of her eyes. After a while she goes to buy cigarettes for us.

She moves easily, with purpose and confidence. As she hands me a cigarette she pushes her gleaming boot hard between my legs. I light the cigarette and ignore Ollie's grinding foot — until she withdraws it slightly — at which point I shift towards her in an attempt to maintain contact. Ollie laughs and stalks onto the dance square.

Ollie's heavy leather jacket lands on my legs. She is wearing one of those work-out vests, revealing the well-defined shoulders of many an hour at the gym. Her body moves like it anticipates every rhythm change, every shock sound and climax. Her energy explodes in all directions.

At some point she lifts me up and we knock against one another in fluid abandon, grounded only by the beat of the music. Ollie grabs the sparse hair above my ears and puts her lips on my neck running her nails down my spine. My legs shake. She smiles proudly when she hears my deep groan. I knee her directly between the legs.

The overhead lights flicker, indicating bed-time. As Ollie heads for the exit a knackered-looking young man with swallows tattooed on his upper arm stretches a hand towards her. She smiles at him and he backs off as he realizes Ollie is a dyke — not a man. He grins at us and moves off.

We laugh and lean towards each other, lips open and eyes questioning, demanding. She raises an eyebrow and runs a forefinger up the inside of my arm.

'You want to spend the night in Waterloo?' I ask, terrified.

'Why not?'

The lights go up fully and the bar staff rush around tables with piles of ashtrays and stacks of glasses. My fingers knead the muscles at the back of Ollie's neck. Her low 'Mmmm' sends a jolt of desire right through me.

'Let's go,' she demands, impatiently.

We drive down the empty London streets and over Waterloo Bridge, turning right at the Old Vic and into my block just south of Waterloo Station. Tonight, I am glad I live alone.

As I attempt to make some tea Ollie lifts my shirt and runs her hands down my sides and across my ribs. She gasps as my nipples harden between her fingers. She kisses and bites below my neck, testing my pain threshhold.

The tea is made and forgotten in a dizzy mingling of limbs. We wrestle each other into submission. Ollie turns my body outside on itself, forcing naked need to surface. Her tongue flicks fast over my molten lips and her haughty nose pressed against my clit sends me into surreal ecstacy. Her hands are strong and she is not afraid to demonstrate their power, gripping and moulding my shoulders, forcing my body to open up to her. Her fingers on my mouth are drenched with our desire. She drives me beyond knowledge or pain. I shake uncontrollably, far beyond stopping the rhythms she has coaxed out of my body. I have lost track of what we are doing. Ollie is gripping me, nails digging into my legs as she shudders on my arm, features contorted.

Later, I am amazed by her tenderness soaping me in the bath, back to the taps with the best of altruism.

'Which of us will run first?' she asks.

I have no answer.

ELEMENTAL HAIKU SEQUENCE

JEWELLE GOMEZ

One

Antherium blood
streaked across your pale, silk thigh.
Answer to desire.

Two

Tiger lily back
beneath my demanding hand
Roundly arched to give.

Three

Gold wheat bends for me,
makes a soft pallet of us.
Leaves no question why.

ROUGH TRADE

SUSIE Q

'Early, early, early in the mornin'
I wake up and I start the yawnin'.
Oh hello, what a very nice day,
but I gotta git up anyway ...'

Miss P rolled over, idly sretching one hand down towards her exhausted fanny. It really had been a hot weekend and getting up meant making it history.

Saturday night, city lights bright through the light drizzle, people stepping across red lights causing the cabbie to curse.

'Drop you here, Miss? You watch yerself, all kind of queer types round here. Area ain't what it used to be, you know. Bulldoze the lot and start again, if I had my way; there's some driftwood round here, I can tell you. Ta love, night.'

P made her way through the damp railway arches and up a spiral stairway that gave out onto a terrace, lit up with neon chinese characters and paper lanterns. This magical contrast to the bleak cityscape always took her breath away, causing her to grow a little taller, push her chest out and renew her resolve that tonight she'd find herself a real hot woman. Looking good was the essence of the thing and P had taken good care with that.

Walking into the mirrored hallway, she was pleased with what she saw. A tight leather mini skirt hugged her backside and a plain black, polo-neck cashmere clung to her full boobs, above which bobbed a chunky, lion's head pendant — not real gold, of course, she was strictly a costume jewellery girl. Her thigh-high, PVC stilletto boots were a new acquisition and showed her legs off well, complimenting the wide belt with extravagant filigree buckle that caught her slim waist. Working out with weights had paid off, she mused, and the instructor was genuine rough trade — shooting her come-on eyes at every opportunity. However, P knew the value of making them wait, so, well pleased — and to be honest, plain turned on — she aimed for the crowded bar area.

Thickset, butch dykes in biker jackets and 501s moved about, supping Pilsners from the can, eyeing up the talent (with difficulty in the low-level lighting that the proprietor favoured). The dance floor, awash with spinning lights, began to fill up as the MC spun some fresh, House sounds. P let the music in and felt the Pils flush through, raising her body heat. When the right track hit the turntable, she was out there getting on down, letting loose the tensions of the week. An initial burst of wild and joyful boogying gradually gave way to pleasurable fatigue — making P's movements sparer but still intensely locked within the rhythm.

As P worked out, she became aware of a prickly heat in her lower back — the kind of heat generated by intense concentration of will from an onlooker. Surreptitiously, she shifted round, panning the groups of women watching the dancers. Sure they were checking her out, in that semi-drunk, casual way that left P unmoved. But there was someone else among them, not yet visible. Just as suddenly as the sensation had begun, it stopped, leaving her confused and somehow needy.

The evening wore on but it had lost that spark. It was obligatory to stay and dance after forking out for cab fares and entrance fees. A couple of girls moved up close but one was spotty and the other was out of it — eyes like pin-points. No, this just wasn't what she had in mind, she thought as she sauntered over to the coat check, biting her lip in disappointment.

About to pass through the mirrorred hall, a light but firm hand gripped her around the elbow, causing P to twist around in surprise and bump forcefully against her captor's chest. Gulping for words to express anger/pleasure, she looked up to see an impassive face studying her with about the same amount of emotion as a butterfly collector struck lucky.

'Who are you?' stammered P, her normally cool manner having fled with the arrival of a prickling sensation knotting her stomach muscles.

'It isn't important who I am, let's just say I'm looking after this place, keeping an eye on things, like you. Quite a goer, aren't you? So I hear.'

Normally P would be angered by such a bald statement but instead she was enthralled by the masterful manner of this woman, compelling her to clarify her reputation as 'a goer.'

'Lady, can you handle it, eh? Wait for me here!'

With that, the large woman swung away from P and threaded her way through the last dancers, overseeing the process of shutting for the night. The place seemed eerie when half empty, the music low now, as the DJ stacked her records into milk crates ready for the ride home.

'Through here,' the woman had reappeared after who knows how long, time having become strangely distorted. A concealed door gave onto a steep fire-escape that led onto a balcony off the floor above. The whole city was mapped out below, street lights making grid patterns suggestive of landing strips. High towers, their flanks lit up with the ever-changing colours of flashverts, pierced the skyline. A chill breeze stirred P's hair and sent a shiver down her spine, as she gazed upon the fitful sleep of the city.

A strong pair of hands snaked around P's waist, shaking off her reverie, securing her firmly to the sturdy woman's groin. The thin leather of her skirt offered little protection against the insistent, grinding movements against her butt. One hand dropped, however, and gripped the exposed thigh flesh immediately below her aching fanny.

This was fast work; the woman already had one hand up her skirt and she didn't even know her name. P gripped the balcony hand-rail and stared straight ahead, wondering whether to offer resistance and then, realizing the woman was far bigger and stronger than she, let the idea slide. Nobody knew she was here, so she was committed to going through with it, whatever 'it' might be. Besides. there was something incredibly erotic about being so out of control. Wasn't it what she'd always wanted, some big, butch dyke to sweep her off her feet and fuck her repeatedly, deaf to any struggling and protestations?

'Roxanne's my name and yours is P, right?'

'Right.'

Roxanne's mouth was close to her ear and now pulled at the flesh of her nape, causing P to wince. Roxanne was unconcerned, concentrating only on devouring P's slender neck.

'I want you now, girl. It's been too long since I had me a hot piece of loving.'

'Mmm,' assented P, at which Roxanne closed her thick fingers around the mound under P's knickers, causing her skirt to pucker around the shape of Roxanne's knuckles. P opened her legs a little wider, willing Roxanne to come inside her with those hard, insistent fingers. On cue, her knickers were eased to one side and eager fingers pulled apart her moist, outer lips. P jumped, as her clit was firmly manipulated and slicked with her own juice. Roxanne had held off penetrating her, seemingly content to dabble barely inside her cunt, leaving P aching for the fucking she felt sure was to follow.

'Let's go inside.' It had started to drizzle. It was hard to walk straight with Roxanne's hand tight against her fanny and the other groping under her bra cup. She was pushed into a darkened apartment, through a living room and directly into a bedroom. The room was lit only by a flashvert glare seeping through drawn venetian blinds and a curious hot wax lamp that formed moulten bubble shapes which rose and collapsed peacefully. Roxanne had closed the door behind them and now turned to face P, forcing her back against the door. This Roxanne was tall and wide, with a short, thick neck. Her dark hair was oiled and slicked back, showing off her square face and determined chin. A grey flannel army shirt hid any curves she might have, and was tucked into well-worn leather jeans that fitted snugly around firm, muscular legs.

P's musings were interrupted by a heavily gold-ringed hand grasping her jaw and tilting her mouth upward towards Roxanne's waiting lips.

'Kiss me,' hissed Roxanne and P parted her lips obligingly to receive Roxanne's thrusting tongue, her jaw aching after a time with the force and intensity of the kiss. Roxanne's hand slipped between P's slippery fanny lips in a rhythmic back and forth motion. Any moment now she would surely come, the rhythm beat stronger and 'Ah!', come she did, as Roxanne forced three, maybe four, fingers straight up her molten cunt. In the bloodrush, she staggered and grabbed Roxanne's leather-clad arse for support.

'You're making me jealous. Kneel down,' growled Roxanne. Without waiting for her to obey (her knees were about ready to buckle anyway), she forced P down until her face was level with Roxanne's flies. P watched as Roxanne slowly undid two buttons and then pulled the zipper to reveal a spongey mass of damp pubic hair. One hand grabbed a handful of P's long hair and forced her mouth onto Roxanne's clit. She gasped for air in between mouthfuls of fanny, eager to feel Roxanne swell inside her. Suddenly leathered thighs clamped around P's head and Roxanne's mound thrust hard into her face in an orgasmic seizure. P held quite still within Roxanne's grip, heady with the fragrance of leather and pussy juice.

P never had had sound knees and was relieved when Roxanne stood back from her, buttoned herself up, allowing P to sink back against the door. Roxanne moved into the shadows and commanded P to lie down on the bed and wait for her. The bed was set low and made up with black bed linen, stained aubergine by the light of the hot wax lamp As P laid her head upon the pillow, she felt herself drifting off, well pleased with the night's events. She hadn't been fucked as such, which was strange since Roxanne seemed the type to give a girl a good going over. Ah well, appearances can be deceiving ....

A feeling of weight aroused the slumbering P, who finally awoke to find Roxanne kissing her nipples, her top and bra having been removed. She could not move, since Roxanne lay on top of her, pinning her down. A hand reached down her thigh and parted wide first one long leg and then the other. Roxanne kissed P deeply, as she slowly removed P's knickers and tossed them to one side. Abruptly, she rolled over for a tub of lubricant and smeared it liberally and lovingly over a handsome strap-on clinched tight about her groin.

'Thought it was over, huh? Did I seem the type to let it go at that, honey? Lie back and relax, feel me and *don't* forget it.'

P felt the cool leather jeans against her naked thighs and Roxanne's weight full upon her once more. Roxanne searched out her mouth and neck while hitching up her skirt and spreading her legs wide, making her more readily available. A rush of air hit her heated fanny as hard hands parted her lips, several fingers snaking inside her preparing the way for the bigger things to come. Roxanne teasingly edged into her outer vagina, letting the head of her shaft bob about here for a while, making P ache for fuller penetration. Her juices bubbled in collusion as P shifted her hips in an attempt to seek a deeper satisfaction. Roxanne laughed at her plight,

'You really want it, huh? Well, here it is!'

And with that she thrust deeply into P, causing her to gasp at the sudden fullness. Her cunt heaved and relaxed, expanding to accommodate the shaft pumping energetically within her. Roxanne partially withdrew, only to lunge deep inside P once more, gripping and raising her arse to aid penetration.

Roxanne was in her element now, giving the girl a thorough seeing to, watching her face as she fucked her hard and fast, sometimes thrusting her tongue in P's mouth roughly when it looked as if the girl was spacing out and forgetting just who was giving it to her. With the strap-on this tight there was no problem coming like this (Roxanne was no 'stone butch'). Just a little more and — oh, there it was! That sweet blood-rush blushing her from head to toe and sending a shudder throughout her muscular frame. Had the chick come too?

Roxanne eased her length out of P's throbbing and well-serviced cunt, the shaft gleaming with her prolific wetness.

'Clean up time, girl!'

P flicked her eyes open in time to see Roxanne lower herself upon P's face and gently pry open her mouth to receive the shaft. Tears sprang up in her eyes as she fought off the urge to gag. Roxanne didn't rush her, evidently thrilled at the sight of P's head bobbing up and down on her cock.

'Now, take it off.'

Roxanne made no move to withdraw, so P had to struggle and squirm to extricate herself. She was further hindered by Roxanne's rough hands squeezing her jiggling tits and pinching the naked flesh of her torso in all the most sensitive areas. It was hard to reach around Roxanne's arse and fumble with the buckles, especially as Roxanne playfully swung her hips causing the dildo to slap against her cheeks, reminding her forcefully of the source of her pleasure.

Roxanne stood over P, one hand on her hip and the other thoughtfully rubbing her crotch area.

'Here,' she threw P her knickers and top, 'I'd better call you a cab. Yeah, tonight you earned your cab fare at least.'

P stood shakily, it hurt to bend over much, nervously smoothing down her hair and making good any damage done.

'Cab's waiting!' announced Roxanne, striding towards the door.

As P turned to go Roxanne spun her around and probed hard within P's aching throat, pushing one hand down into her damp knickers and penetrating her a final time. P sighed and laid a hot cheek against the rough material of Roxanne's shirt, not wanting to break the embrace, endeavouring to savour the fullness in her cunt.

'Remember me, darlin'. I enjoyed having you very much.'

The city lights twinkled against the pallor of the blood red breaking dawn, empty streets slipping by in anonymous uniformity. P smiled at her tired reflection in the misty window, shifting her arse in remembrance.

'Early, early, early in the mornin'
I wake up and I start the yawnin'
You know how chicken
is always finger-lickin'?
Well, let me tell you babe
this shit is stickin'!'

APPLES WITH ROSIE

JO SMITH

The village boys would shout, 'Hey, Apple Rosie' as she walked to the orchard with her light wicker baskets and heavy apple breasts bobbing with the swing of her arms. She would blush angrily at the call and hug her baskets round herself, or sometimes swing proudly on; but whatever her reaction the boys would spend the next few idle minutes discussing how ripe and ready for plucking she was.

A first evening's cool breeze at last brushed her legs under the heavy skirt she caught the apples in. Rosie let the last apple she'd reached for fall far below her. The other pickers had already left for home, and she was the last, still climbing and lost in a daydream. She twisted round now, and comfied herself in a crook of branches. Stretching back with her head buried in a leafy branch, she let her eyes wander up into the skirts of the apple tree, where she saw, way out of reach, apples too far to gather, and hidden birds, and nests and mostly leaves. She closed her eyes and let her hand wander down to her breast, holding it hard but gently, pushing the little crab apple nipple into her palm with her thumb. Her breasts were heavy and soft — like two huge ripe apples bursting to be gathered, she thought smiling, to be cupped in two strong hands, to be lifted and weighed lovingly in two soft hands ....

She picked two apples, having to pull herself up heavily to reach them, and sat back again, holding them against her breasts. Her right hand let one apple slip and slide down to hold her rounded stomach, plump and soft under her skirts. Feet braced on wider branches, she felt the flower between her legs open out.

A slight rustling underneath her made her heart jump and she lay still, taut, waiting, open and wet, and waiting, and wet. The movement below stopped, teasing her, waiting for her panic or frenzy. Then she felt a cold hard thrust under her buttocks. Someone was rolling an apple along the crack of her buttocks to meet the slow trickle of wet that dripped down it. Rosie sat on it hard and pushed her arse into it slowly. The apple travelled up and began massaging her wet cunt. It rolled round and round slowly, spinning out her pleasure, and she pushed into it hard and long, letting herself relax and lie back on the branch. When she came she shuddered, and the tree shuddered with her, waving its boughs as she let her great strong legs ripple with the orgasm. Long fingers opened and stroked her cunt as lips kissed and sucked it in.

The branches below shook again, and Rosie watched as Sal, with her defiant gait, long legs striding, held a large rosy apple in her bony fingers and munched and sucked on it as she walked away.

DON'T PUT YOUR DAUGHTER ON THE BOTTLE, MRS BYRNE

HILARY WEST

She's sucked everything in sight
— her hand, my neck,
the teddy —
she's crying now
desperately, eyes screwed tight
mouth wide
her lips won't close on what's offered
She wants it all
the teat, the bottle-neck
no half-measures
yet all that's too much
for her hungry mouth
— only the breast will do

She's worn out all distractions
— work, conversation,
the ever-faithful bottle
she heads towards the bar
like a baby to the nipple
But the beer is flat
she finds no edge
I tease her with the taste of it
over the phone
I know it's not enough
she'll soon be round because
only the breast will do

LUNCH WITH CARLA

ANNA MARIE SMITH

I saw Carla in the library today. I watched her from the other side of the cutlery dispenser; she remained immersed in a spirited discussion with her friends. She hadn't changed at all.

We had worked together on a government-sponsored research project three summers ago when she was nineteen and curious about feminism. The project was located in this uptight research centre with a dozen anal retentive secretaries and seven smart-ass executives. We were assigned a windowless, airless office the size of two double beds. The three of us, Carla, another researcher, Suzanne and I, were never really accepted. We would all arrive late, in ripped jeans and punked-out t-shirts, comparing real and sometimes imagined hangovers in loud voices. We didn't have our own phone, so we'd invade one of the empty executive suites, and gossip with our friends, switching from French to English, and in Carla's case, to Spanish.

Suzanne and I soon found ourselves getting involved in Carla's tumultuous life. She always seemed to be rescuing one of her friends from some crisis or another. At any given moment, she would be making a call to her boyfriend to arrange for some hash for the weekend, or to the woman from Guatemala hiding out from immigration, or another to her friend from Paris who had become pregnant while travelling across the States. Listening to her passionate voice, I became enthralled.

I suppose in the end we basically terrorized the rest of the staff, and, since I was in charge of the project, I couldn't be fired, and Carla and Suzanne weren't about to complain about me. Every day, we would get these memos about our conduct, dress, lunch hours, telephone bills, xerox accounts and coffee mugs. They were always typed on brightly-coloured paper, in different executive shades. So we did creative things with them, Japanese cut-outs, collages and mobiles, and added them to the wall where we had taken down the two insipid silkscreens. By the end of the summer, we had constructed an entire multi-media installation piece, with our cut outs, polaroids, balled up lengths of typewriter corrector ribbon, and broken glass. The secretaries complained but it was our office. Putting Carla on a research team was like asking Patti Smith to be a bank teller, and I wanted to keep her amused.

We usually ate our sandwiches in the office, leaving us a good hour and a half for a lunch break outside the centre. That summer, like every other Toronto summer, was incredibly warm and humid. Suzanne hated the sun so she would do her shopping in her break. Carla loved the heat. She'd wear the skimpiest t-shirt possible, and one of those flowing cotton skirts dyed black with the frayed edges. We'd walk to the park down the road, towards the outdoor swimming pool, and feed each other plums and cherries.

We'd pass through the locker area in the women's section and strip off our clothes. Carla had, and still has, a gorgeous body. Deeply tanned, solid shoulders and muscular arms, full, rounded breasts and swimmer's thighs. She'd unhook her skirt and swing out of it in one easy motion, and scratch her pubic hair unselfconsciously. Chatting to me all the while, she'd raise her arms, exposing her wonderfully hairy pits and pull her top off, stretching and teasing her muscles. She never seemed to notice the way I watched her. Then we'd laugh, slap each other with our towels, and head for the pool. I'd do about ten lengths and flop down on the poolside to watch her alternate between butterfly and breast-stroke, clearing a sure path amongst the bobbing and the screaming neighbourhood kids.

One of those was a little girl who loved to try to float while holding on to the edges of the pool. On one afternoon, she was really upset, carrying on in a panicked stream of Portuguese and English about her mother not picking her up on time. Carla scooped her up, and, with reassuring Spanish words, carried her towards the change room. I followed, with towels and sunglasses, and the girl's tiny pair of running shoes. By the time I reached the showerstalls, the girl was already laughing, pulling on Carla's long black hair. Carla held her confidently, cradling her easily in her strong arms. The little girl giggled and smiled as Carla set her down and gently soaped and rinsed their bodies in the shower spray. There was a shriek of happiness as an older Portuguese woman in skirts and shopping bags appeared in the doorway, and, after quickly scrambling into a yellow shorts and top set, the little girl was gone.

I turned to Carla, and then she noticed that I had been watching her. I looked down, stepped out of my damp Speedo, and hung my towel on the rail of the shower stall next to hers. I turned the water on and she yelled, 'Fuck around, you're getting all the hot, ya silly bitch!' She had stepped out of her stall towards mine. I turned and looked into her eyes, hesitated, then slowly reached to run my hand down from her throat to her slippery smooth belly. She stared back, and then somehow we were both in the one stall, curtained off from the empty shower room.

'Well, boss, is this a business meeting, or what?' She always did have a weird sense of humour.

'Depends what you're into right now, chica.'

You know those moments when you are in such an intense mood that you feel so incredibly turned on and almost faint at the same time — we had one of those moments then, bodies inches away from each other in the wetness, hands finally touching with almost electric shock. I leaned back against the cool wall and waited for her. Her hesitant touch moved towards my thighs. She looked at me once more for a second and then bent slowly to her knees, her hands following the curves of my lower back and ass, her tongue tentatively kissing my belly, the outlines of my hair, the folds of my cunt. Her grip on my ass became firmer as she found my clit, and I came gently moments later. The water continued to pour relentlessly down on her back as she kneeled there, breathing hard. I reached down to caress her face and gently helped her up.

She smiled at me shyly and murmured, 'Wow ... different.'

'You mean it's your first time?'

She nodded.

I moved my arms to encircle her back. She began to close her eyes. I drew her face towards me and I reached and finally kissed her. She kissed back and held me tighter. We folded our legs between each other, and I helped her to ride my thigh, squeezing and pulling wet skin. We ran our fingers hungrily around each other's nipples, kissing, tonguing harder.

'Turn around,' I whispered into her ear, dodging the warm water spray.

She turned automatically leaned on the other wall, moving her legs apart, raising her ass towards me just a little. I turned the spray to wash down her ass and her thighs, as I ran my other hand down her back. I wished that I could have prolonged the next move all afternoon, but I knew that we only had a few minutes. I leaned closer towards her and lightly massaged her ass, gently and slowly, probing her labia, parting her with a forefinger, playing wih the smooth wetness of her labia, and easing two fingers into her vagina. As her wetness closed in around me, I felt a rush of warmth. Maybe now her passion included me, maybe now she would think of me as someone special, maybe she could introduce me to her friends.

I'd have to make the apartment more interesting. My sisters could lend me some tapes and clothes.

I pressed myself up against her back, my mouth on her neck. Listening to the pattern of her breathing, I stroked her gently. She began to open up to me, and I slipped more in.

'I want you to control this yourself,' I said into her ear. 'Touch yourself, make yourself come. I'll hold you and rock you as hard and as fast as you want.'

She hesitated and then reached down towards her cunt, and I could feel her rubbing fingertips colliding with mine. I kept on stroking and holding her firmly, kissing and sucking on her neck. She pushed a little further back and we became locked in an increasing rhythm. Her breathing became moaning, and the moaning became a string of Spanish words. The pressure on my wrist became almost unbearable. With a shudder her body finally gave up, and I held her close as she was gripped in a long thrusting orgasm. I eased my tired fingers out of her cunt, kissing her neck, stroking her hair, waiting for her to speak. She turned.

'I like you and that was great, but I don't love you.'

I tried to react as if I could handle the distance.

'Listen, we can talk later. Let's go back to work.' We kissed for the last time, and I turned off the water and reached for my towel.

THAT TIMELY NUANCE

MARNIA MONTAGUE

WENDY

Soft, so soft. Could have walked around a looming, grey, old building. Pitted holes, cracking structure, cold wind causing whooshing sounds inside, through broken, hanging hingings. A giant has scooped out holes in the floor for sandcastles. Leaving obstacle course debris about the rubbish dune rooms. There's a bat under the stairwell and a rat in the lard. Could have circled that building again and again and from the slightest crevice, it would come. Emanating, undulating, like the Bisto scent, toward my nose. There I turn, enter, and walk up. There et lay, in wait for me. My Sleeping Beauty, who did not shut eye/me out, denying the bliss, but offered gentle smile, able for a kiss. Arms not slack and dead by your side, but reached behind to support your head. So pushing down chin into neck just a little to give you that so grown up look.

'Am I allowed to?' wondered Sherone. 'Am I allowed?' Nothing is moving outside, just the wind. And the fighting Sun, having won this round, is streaming through a split lace curtain, down onto a buttoned, white blouse.

'Am I allowed to?' wondered Sherone as et reached a tentative hand forward. No encouragement. No displeasure. A gentle smile. First button. Touch, touch, touch. Skin so soft. Second button. Third button. Little brown hands reach in to find the colours at the end of the rainbow. There are mahogany, varnished table-tops, there are Bourneville chocolates, there is a wedding ring gold. There are all the colours of the rainbow and more in this warm/hard, butter-skin, though the clouds may win this next.

So from *here* the source. From here the undulations. Curve my palm about your curve. Bare breasts, nipple tip hard, so inviting. Smooth. Sherone's hands smoothed a breast each, to rise, rising, to peak. Flowing and sliding down the other side. Following each other around, taking turns at leader. Here a rise, there a curve. Ah look, round here, a dimple. Twiddle, twiddle, the nipples. No movement. Gentle smile. Sherone loved those breasts. And never forgot that exploration. Et had never before come so close to discovering etu future. Not a cross word exchanged throughout. Not a word indeed. Just a sweet smile, dark brown, magical/swollen/warmth quality. The rainbow won the day.

LINDA

'Have you played doctors & nurses before?' Linda lay a bed but one from Sherone.

'Yeah, I did once.'

'How old were you?'

'I was six, or seven, I think.'

'Who was it with?'

'My cousin. And et was thirteen.'

'Cor.'

'Have you done it with anyone before?'

'Nah — yeah actually, I do it with me sister sometimes but ...'

Silence.

'Shall we do it?' They say it together, each wishes they hadn't, then glad they did.

'You come to my bed.'

'Ah na-ah. You come to mine. I said it. I said it.' Sherone sucked etu teeth and folded back the bed cover slowly. By the light of the moon and corridor bulb, et easily made etu way to Linda's bed, with its pink counterpane. There was a tense moment when they realized how clearly they could see each other, so that Linda's cue for turning back etu bedsheet, became Linda cuddling it up to etu chin. Sensitive Sherone, well-trained in the gentle smile, reached up unhurriedly to stroke Linda's hand and bring down the cover. Linda looked on, hypnotized.

'I wanted this done on me,' realized Sherone, receiving an unexpected pang of disappointment for etu discovery. But Linda lay, anticipating. So Sherone began unbuttoning Linda's nightshirt.

'I'll just have to inspect you now. This won't take long. Take it off. Ooh dear, lay back down now. And what do we have here then?'

Sherone tweaked a nipple. Linda closed etu eyes and moaned, twisting etu head, like et'd seen them do in films. This started Sherone's heart banging with more than mere excitement and et began running etu hands up and down Linda's creamy, white body.

'Must check for blisters now mustn't we. What did you say — you got burnt?'

Linda tossed and moaned a little more but not enough to bring the staff in. Then taking Sherone's hand, et pushed it down into etu pyjama bottoms, turning it, rather frantically, the whole time, over the hairless skin. Now Sherone, mesmerized, watched Linda's face as et managed to wiggle a finger into the hole. It felt rough in there. The forehead scrunched up, the eyes closed tight, the mouth pushed forward, the moans, the cries, the twisting head, the moon and the darkness on the flat, white chest, the rough hole, the ... knock at the door.

Sherone leaped over the other bed and into etu own, not even conscious of having separated from Linda. Who was hugging etu counterpane again to etu chin and in a sweet, whiney voice asking, 'Wha-at?'

'What you two girls doing in there?' Danny from the next door boys' room tried to imitate an adult mun's growl, failed dismally and ran away shrieking.

MAURA

Maura was the newest addition to the children's home and Sherone's bestest friend. Et supposed that Linda would have been, only after two years, etu mum had signed the adoption papers. Sherone shrugged. Maura sat across the table slapping at Danny's hand. 'I don't like playing doctors and nurses with you lot, so just stop it will you.'

'Yeah, that's what I fink.' Sherone helped fet out. 'You've got all those dangly bits, and you always force our hand down.'

'Yeah, or you give us something stupid. Like a cigarette. And I don't even smoke yet.'

Sherone gazed at the ceiling. 'I think I'll start smoking when I'm twelve. Two years to go.'

'Oh for fuck's sake.' Maura pushed back etu chair, knocking it over.

Sherone was always surprised at etu language. Et was only four months older after all. But apparently etu mother was an alcoholic prostitute.

'Paki,' snapped an embarrassed Danny. Maura's skin had the slightest brown colour to it. The girls left the dinner table and went to their room. Maura threw fetself onto the bed next to Sherone's.

'Did you used to play doctors and nurses with Linda?'

'What do you know?' Sherone bent to find non-existent white socks under the bed and hide etu face.

'Linda told me.'

'Linda lied.'

'Would you play it with me?' Just like Maura that was. But sweet Sherone, gentle smile, sensitive, could understand that. Et prepared fetself to turn, stand and explore again those smooth and rough spots. When to etu amazement, et felt Maura's hands come round to encircle etu waist and chest from behind. Because Maura had extra weight on, et wore a mini bra and now Sherone could feel the flaccid protrusions from etu chest, pressing into etu own back. Sherone turned to find a newer, softer, face upon Maura. The two girls giggled and touched the night away.

DEONNE

'Ah ah ah, you're doing it too hard.'

Deonne released Sherone's cunt mound and searched again quickly for the lost lips. Fastening a pout to Sherone's heavy, breathing mouth, et pressed hard and poked etu tongue in and out. Sherone carried on rubbing hard and fast between Deonne's legs, meanwhile trying to catch Deonne's tongue with etu own. Et rolled etu body on top of Deonne's then continued the hard, fast action, now on the rough ceiling, now on the pulsing clit. Deonne squeezed etu eyes, put etu hands onto Sherone's shoulders and started their bodies in an alternative up/down motion, so pressing young, budding breasts, *hard* against each other, tearing nipples. Deonne's nipples were so rocky, discovered Sherone. Just like Deonne. And now et could feel Deonne turning them both over, sinking two fingers into Sherone's suddenly aching cunt.

'Oooaah.'

Sherone ground onto them, turning etu hips, pressing etu tough arse into the bed, then whipping back up onto Deonne's fingers. So fast. So wet. Deonne was kissing etu tits again now.

'Oh God.'

Licking them. Kissing them. Sherone hung onto Deonne's back, separated fingers, tense. So wet. So wet. Then et found Deonne's cunt again. By this time, it was dripping. Hard and fast, like et seemed to prefer it. Deonne pushed it away, withdrew etu fingers, put one leg between Sherone's two and they bucked and kissed for the last few minutes, then lay sweating and panting.

'Shall we have a cigarette?'

Deonne had everything Sherone didn't have. Etu own room, lighter skin, a mum and dad *and* sister *and* brother. And et had the cigarettes. But Sherone was the faster runner. Deonne sparked the match.

'When's your birthday?'

'I'm going to be thirteen on March fourth.'

'Really? Guess what. I'm going to be thirteen on March tenth.' Et took a little inhalation, blew it out, passed the fag to Sherone. Sherone took a lug and blew it straight out. Deonne watched fet.

'Why did your mum call you Sherone?'

'Cos et said that most Sharons were herots and when et said Sharon, it came out Sheron anyway, so it ended up Sherone.'

Deonne, looking mystified, took back the cigarette, lugged it once, then stubbed it out for the morning. That night, they slept top to toe, as always. Come the morning, as Deonne sparked up again, et began,

'Last night ...' drag, puff. Sherone's heart did the tortoise then the hare. 'Did you want to?'

Sherone thinks carefully, decides et isn't sure of the answer, so plays it safe as can be.

'I did it because I thought you wanted to.' They are viewing each other from the sides of their eyes.

'And I did it because I thought you wanted to.' Their eyes are mistrustful slits. They both know it mustn't happen again. They both know that neither can tell. Though right now, they're not sure of the reasons why.

◆ ◆ ◆

Glossary

Wem ... Woman
Mun ... Man
Wim ... Women
Min ... Men
Et ... She
Therefore, princess = *princet/princut*
Ut ... He
Ot ... Either
Fet ... Her
Fut ... Him
Etu ... Hers
Sut ... His
Etfema ... Female
Utfema ... Male
Etine ... Feminine
Utine ... Masculine
Maisstot ... Master
Perot ... Person
Humot ... Human (silent 't')

WATER BEASTS

BERTA R FREISTADT

You make me a sea lion
We are sea-beastly
Together.
Water light reflects
On your shell breasts
Which soft, drop
Stalacmite
As we sport straight faced
But sweet,
As we hump and gasp
As we snort and swoon
We are two hippos agog
In our water circus,
We make tides fall
And rise to our moon.
You are limpet mouthed
Waves wet your black hair,
Will you drown for me?

EXERCISING RESTRAINT

BARBARA SMITH

For Beccy

We both have lovers already, in fact we are both in love, but for reasons known only to us (and perhaps therefore still unknown), we have decided to launch ourselves upon this voyage of exploration. So we exchanged probing initiations some weeks back and now find ourselves in my home, contemplating Sunday lunch.

We talk for hours, barely acknowledging what is happening between us, except to admit that we are taking turns to hassle the other and excite an uncomfortable tension. I wonder what is going on: you appear combative, but with a smile that leaves the intention ambiguous.

Position one: We sit primly on my bed-settee, side by side and untouching, you at your end, me at mine. When you get up to change a record, I slither forward full-length on my belly and watch you bending over the albums. My head is to one side, slightly off the edge of the settee: am I trying to look coy, seductive, provocative, what? I want you to turn round and catch me lusting after your arse, gazing up at you through long lashes, I want you to be completely overwhelmed by my desire for you. I want you to come over here, fuck the arse off me on my belly, forgetting all your promises to yourself. Push my face down into the settee, tower above and behind me, raise my arse in the air, and fuck me with a hard hand. I don't understand your resistance, your restraint. I don't understand why wanting is not enough for doing. I am lying here on my belly, naked under my clothes, and I just want you to take me and fuck the consequences.

For the moment, though, a precious line separates us and makes us safe. *But the contradiction* — the first of many to come — is that we have already overstepped that line of safety. You have entered my home. I have invited you in, to penetrate the inner me only known to close friends and lovers. And what have you done? Welcome to my snare, said the catcher caught for once.

This is a home for single occupancy only. Two rooms with a life-style divided between, I leave my head in one room and my body in the other. Room One: a bedsitting room, for fucking, sleeping and dreaming. Room Two: a study, for thinking, rationalizing, analyzing and writing about what happens in Room One. No room for anyone to have an existence independent of me. The bed dominates the only room you are allowed to enter, and, whether bed or settee, it is where I do my fucking merging transformation of the visitor absorbed.

My opening line, some weeks previous: 'Do you fuck around?'

Trying to shock you, perhaps, make you swoon with a dangerous kind of knowing.

Your answer: 'Well, I can fuck around — if I want.'

On another occasion, sitting on the pavement outside the pub, I am drunk. You arrive late, looking around for me in a cool kind of way, as if not really looking but still hoping I'm already there.

I'm high on chance meetings and mild flirtations with strangers, and I say to you: 'Give us a kiss,' still trying the old shock-'em-into-submission line.

And you say: 'No, I'm not going to fuck with you. I want to be responsible for once.'

I think: You mean you can't handle monogamy. I say: 'Responsible to whom?'

Undaunted and in perfect control you reply: 'Myself'.

I am undone, caught out, can only comment, 'I'm glad you said that. Thinking, however, 'Bastard, why won't you play with me? I'm the older woman, you're the young one supposed to be flattered by my attention, admiring of my sophistication, my knowing of the world. But you, young woman, younger than my lover who is young enough as it is, you put me in my place. I think you think: Fuck the years, fuck the experience, fuck all the fucking you've done. I won't be cowed by you, the way others might be, I might still be impressed by you but the important thing is that impressed is impressing.

So I realize I can't manipulate you, can't make you dare the way the others do. I'm intrigued.

Side by side then, we're not really making small talk and yet not even talking about sex. Like everyone else, for the moment at least, we are talking about talking about sex. *I'm* doing the talking, in fact, trying to explain my problems with butch-femme, trying to explain a dream I had about my lover, a story I was trying to write, where I wailed some deep, primal scream and am again on the point of repeating the tears. And you listen, take it all in, and I wonder what you make of me. Are you really hearing while you listen? Does it matter?

I think: You only want the sound of my voice, the depth of my emotion, the depths rather than the superficial meanings I attach to words, the *sound* of passionate words rather than the words themselves. But there is some deeper connection, something I know is happening, sense is happening, can feel happening in my cunt.

Position two: Something breaks my concentration and I accidentally lean against your leg. You say, so simply: 'That's the first time you've touched me since I got here.' This is hours later. I feel challenged, almost reprimanded with (what I hope is) your disappointment. I wonder what is holding me back, why you always wait for me to make the first move and why I almost feel you sit in judgement on me even though my every move is the right one.

I remember that time, in another pub, I had watched you dancing with some animal-like power. I watched you and refused to join in, despite your request, because watching was what I wanted, to have that power over you, the power to watch and not to share with you. The power not to touch.

You were hot and sweaty, so hot you had to remove your leather jacket — it was the first time I had seen you without it — and I could have sworn that it had been grafted onto your skin. And there you were, without your skin, dancing and moving and sweating, knowing I was watching you.

I was about to go and you said there was something you wanted to say to me. You didn't want to fuck with me, but you wanted to touch me, to be physically close to me. It was unexpected, powerful. My cunt clenched. This beautiful animal wanted to be physically close to me. This powerful creature had shed her skin for me, to make my cunt run with her sweat, had gone naked in public for me. For me.

(Oh baby, she was just *hot* that's all.)

We went and sat somewhere quiet. I said: I feel the same way too. I explained my initial attraction and then said it had changed, moved from the initial superficial similarities to my lover to something completely different. Something that belonged to her. And then, claiming drunkenness as my alibi, I said I must go, and then impetuously kissed her mouth.

Her mouth.

Just thinking of your mouth now has made my cunt clench again. Your soft, receptive, hungry mouth, much wider than mine, which could swallow me up and yet respects my smallness. Moist, uninhibited, yet waiting for the invitation. And like a prat I get embarrassed, think I have already overstepped the mark, have made a sexual contact which you didn't want. So I rush out without looking back or saying goodbye. I think I am so daring, so sexual, so in control, so assertive, so *butch*, but you control me all the time. You swallow up all my bravado and spit me out with ease.

So, to your question some paragraphs back, I reply: 'You could have touched me?'

But that was not the point. And why the question mark? All you have to do is sit there, because you know my restlessness will give you all you want.

Position three: Having sat, so prim and proper, equals perhaps, now we are both full-length, stretched out, feet by head, legs side by side. Differentiated, opposite, lined up for another battle. The light is behind me (and I know how that looks to you, my head so dark but surrounded by a halo) and you, at the far end of the room, bathed in darkness and squinting slightly to see me better, you are playing with my feet. You embrace my legs.

You say: 'I just want to hold onto you.'

And I have no idea what you're thinking but it doesn't matter. My feet become my cunt.

I carry on talking, feel like I am wittering on, feel that you are still not interested in what I am saying as much as the sounds that come out and the fact that my noisy busy-ness means you can be silent.

Your silence becomes a magnet, and even though I know in other circumstances I would be interesting, here and now it doesn't really matter what I say. You want the biggest distance between us to draw us together. My sound, your silence, means you can study me in a way that no mirror will reveal. You are taking me to pieces, examining me like a watch with the back off, and I feel like I am being undressed and flayed alive. You crawl under my skin while I'm not watching, but I need to keep talking, keep sounding, because silence, your silence, will draw me in, demolish the distance between us which has made the encounter safe so far. If I fall silent too, you will pick me up and put me in your pocket.

I'm trying to explain that I have problems with monogamy, and add meaningfully, also with non-monogamy. It was meant to be an almost joke. But you just carry on peeling back my skin with your dark eyes, squinting and as small as olive pits. I catch my breath as you catch my glance. I clench my teeth as my cunt grabs my attention again. Try to continue.

I'm trying to explain why I'm not going to fuck you (hadn't I heard what you said before? You're not going to fuck me!), not a matter of 'if' but 'when' because now the time is not right. I'm trying to be so right-on and adult about this.

'Look, I really want to fuck you but I just can't at the moment.' (Sorry, baby).

And you say: 'But we've been fucking all afternoon. I'm in your home, you've cooked me a lovely meal, and that's fucking.'

I parade through my life for you. My past life, so rational and rationalized now, is open to your gaze. Of course, you will see things about me I will never see, others will never see. You will know things about me that words cannot capture, that you cannot tell *me*. Your gaze is of the cruel scientist about to dissect. And I am still drawn in, like a rat caught in the cobra's gaze. A tantalizing split-second from death, frozen in the lover's embrace that becomes a strangulation. Caught, suspended. And yet you will not fuck me.

I can't cope. I feel as if I'm running downhill, always slightly ahead of where I want to be, where I can feel safe and unassailable. Your presence makes me nervous in a delicious way, injects me with your power. I study you. You're not really the strong silent type, though strong *and* silent. Not the mean, moody, broody type that hides a vacuum. You wait for me to exhaust my encyclopaedic book-learnt knowledge and then demolish the overblown edifice with one simple, direct line.

'Come up here I want to hold you.'

And like a good little girl, I comply. I add this to my list of what does not constitute a fuck.

I nestle my head against your breast and wonder why your nipple is not hard when I am near enough to enclose it. My head is on your heart, I move with your lungs, I breathe your breath, I know you are excited but you do not move. You really do just want to hold me.

I am beginning to think I don't understand at all. Why is your strong hard body not crumbling because I am so close? Why is your breath not quickening, your back not arching? Why is your breast not straining to assault my mouth with want? Here am I, on the precipice of desire, on the tips of my toes, looking down and feeling dizzy with the height of it all, and there are you, so cool, so in control, so turned on and yet turning in.

Position four: I sit up. I can't stand to be this close and unmoving, unmerging. Why are our bodies still separate? I go back down to my end of the settee: damn you, I want *you* to move for a change.

I forget now how this happened, but suddenly we are both down the same end of the settee. Fuck you for making me wait so long. But at last, at least, we're touching. You sit me between your legs, both of us facing the same way now as if astride some monstrous motorbike.

'Lean back,' you say. 'Lean your weight against my body.'

So I do, at a slight angle, my head thrown back, my neck slightly exposed.

Now I *am* lost. Now my life rushes down the centuries and the here-and-now has gone forever. I am every woman who has ever been, who has ever nearly been fucked, nearly had an orgasm, nearly got the thing she holds most dear — the restoration of her integrity. I am nearly there.

Your legs, outside mine, your feet hooked in and around my legs. My head thrown back, my body supported by yours. Your body is the altar upon which I will be willingly sacrificed. I am caught, taut, stretched and tensed like a watch spring, uncoiled, no recoil, a spring with no spring.

You top me from the bottom, you smart-arse cow, but so, so clever. You have manoeuvred me into the most perfect balance, the most delicious contradiction, on top but bottom, and I can feel the paradox welling in my chest. Then, icing on the cake, you grab my wrists and place them on your legs. And, candles on the cake, your head leans forward, your nose alongside my ear, and you breathe your passion into me.

Stop the clock. Don't breathe. Hold your breath and see what happens. Your grip of my wrists, a millimetre at a time, becomes stronger, more enclosing. Your breath quickens now, fills my ear with your demands and my ear becomes my cunt.

And what about my cunt? Poor baby, lying there unattended, focus of all the whirling swirling coming over me. So much inner movement but outside I am absolutely motionless. I dare not move. In other circumstances my back would be arching now against your breasts, my body would be moving with yours against yours, the small of my back would be grinding into your cunt, your cunt that I can feel is so wet it is almost dissolving itself. It's all in my head, you're fucking my head.

This is almost like a death, one of those out-of-body experiences when I can look down upon myself, watch us caught in this trap of unmoving, see a shadow slink out of your cunt and sit triumphantly between my legs like a wicked Peter Pan come home to roost. The spiralling rattles inside my brain, the way, as a child, I imagined Alice fell down the rabbit-hole. The negotiation of our powers has created a vortex, sucked in, suspended, everything stands still. Breathing so hard, in time with each other, *but the contradiction is that we are holding our breath.* I am completely pinioned by your gripping of my wrists, *but the contradiction is that your imprisoning of me imprisons you also.* You dare not move. Not an inch, not a millimetre. Each breath must come together. To move even slightly out of synchrony will break the spell, will begin the body-fuck.

My cunt is exposed now, yet sheathed by my exterior so you cannot penetrate my body. I am desperate for you to touch my cunt, which is so hot but at the same time I can feel a cool breeze, like toothpaste minty hot and menthol cold. Icy blast upon my cunt. Fuck me with your clever paradox. No connection of skin. My brain becomes my cunt, and you fuck me good sweetheart.

My brain has caved in upon itself. Head moved into the body room, something slithered down my spine to that deep part of me that only seems activated the night before I bleed, the part of me only touched by the deepest, hardest fucking, and I start to laugh, the way I laugh after coming, that is when I haven't wept after coming, and only now can I settle back into the curves of your body and stop the tensing ache.

SHE MADE NO SOUND

STORME WEBBER

she made no sound as she turned, only the changing of the
shape of space around her and the sound that it made in my
mind was all. the night was hot and it slowed our words
made them hang sticky in the air. i was doubly affected,
women who are beautiful to me always distract my thoughts.

she was speaking; i was watching her mouth her teeth her
tongue moving not listening ...

i am a woman who likes to play with words, change and rearrange
them to say exactly what i want said but at times i refuse
to deal with them. their reality is too abstract when what
i want is to feel my skin as close as possible to your
skin — when what i need is a feeling not a thought.
no words, please, thank you.

anyway lady is still talking — meanwhile i've fallen into
her mouth am about to go down for the last time when she
jerks me back to this room and reality: 'you're not even
listening!!'
'o yeah baby yes i'm hearing what you said only on a
much different level you see ...'
& i can't help it i'm grinnin like a fool
waiting for you to smile back
an you do
and again
we change the shape of space around us
and no more words, please. thank you.

THE SHEBA EDITORS

Michelle McKenzie has worked at Sheba for the past three years. She also works in community development. She loves her work and friends and wants to spend more time at home and travelling.

Araba Mercer is now into her fourth year at Sheba and cannot think of anything else she would rather do. She also works part-time for Health Rights and until recently was involved with the Black Lesbian and Gay Centre project. She has recently discovered the joys of living alone, and does so in south London.

Sue O'Sullivan has been at Sheba for five challenging and exciting years. Now she is in the process of making changes in her life which include leaving Sheba and finding new ways to work and relax. Can Sue find happiness without Sheba? Will anything else fulfill her in the same way? Such is the mystery of life!

CONTRIBUTORS' BIOGRAPHIES

Tina Bays

After having a first time ever story published in *Serious Pleasure,* Tina Bays is thrilled that her second attempt is included in this book. Her erotic fiction is firmly rooted in the late night fantasy genre; fun as it is, she'd like to develop more sophisticated story writing skills.

Julie A Bennett

I was born in Portsmouth in 1954 and came from a working class background. I'm a lesbian and I started writing poetry as a way of expressing my feelings and exploring different facets of myself. It is very personal and I find I write mainly very late at night when my barriers are down and emotions high. All my poetry is written from personal experiences. My other interests are photography, art, Shiatsu, healing, and women's poetry.

Alissa Blackman

Alissa Blackman is an Ashkenazi Jew who was born in 1969 in the borough of Manhattan, New York. She attends a small college in the Midwest where she secretly hopes organizing the lesbigay community will turn out being fun as well as being politically worthwhile. She enjoys Saran Wrap, green latex, and accidental sublimation through struggle for social change.

Jeannie Brehaut
Jeannie Brehaut was born in Toronto, Canada in 1963. She lives in London and works as a waitress. Jeannie has written short stories, essays, poetry and is currently working on a novel. Her work has appeared in the *Pink Paper*, *Aurora* magazine and *Delighting The Heart: A Notebook by Women Writers*, The Women's Press, 1989. Her poetry is coming out in a lesbian anthology soon to be published by The Oscars Press.

Fiona Cooper
Fiona Cooper regularly writes for the *Pink Paper*. Her first two novels are *Rotary Spokes* and *Heartbreak on the High Sierra*. She lives in Tyneside and is head over heels in love and nothing else matters.

Rosie Cullen
Born in Dublin and lived many places since. I'm a playwright, who has written for companies as disparate as the Royal Shakespeare Company, Little Women, Electric, and Solent People's Theatre, plays for both adults and children. Currently, working on a couple of screenplays, studying for an MA in Film and TV Scriptwriting, and part-time writer in residence at a psychiatric hospital. This is my first short story to be published.

Eleanor Dare
I was educated in London (Barbara Woodhouse method), and have always lived there. I am nearly twenty-five. If I had more confidence I would call myself a painter and writer, but I am really almost an assistant librarian.

Linda Devo
Linda Devo is twenty years old, of which the first thirteen were spent in Ghana. She is a black lesbian mother, a Buddhist, an engineering student and an Aries. She also sits on the management committee of the Lesbian Archives. The loves of her life are her bike, music, reading and flirting. This is her first published short story; she has stacks more in the same line if anyone's interested.

Jo Fisk
Born in New York, 1963, Jo Fisk is a lawyer musician and writer living and working in London.

Berta R Freistadt
Berta R Freistadt is a Londoner. Nothing has changed much in her life since *Serious Pleasure*. The bemusement she felt then at being included in that volume is nothing to the sheer incredulity she feels at being in *More Serious*

Pleasure. Her entry is of course fraudulent, since the sort of pleasure referred to in this book, serious or otherwise, has long been absent from her life. Indeed the poems printed here were written so long ago that she can scarcely remember writing them, let alone who they were written about. She represents a forgotten and, of course, very oppressed minority — RERC (Retrospectively Erotic Reluctant Celibates).

Jewelle Gomez
Jewelle Gomez is the author of *Flamingoes and Bears*, a collection of poetry. Her first novel, *The Gilda Stories*, will be published by Firebrand Books (Spring 1991). She has been an activist in movements against gender, race and class oppression for twenty years. Originally from Boston, she currently lives in Brooklyn, NY, with Maisie and the spirits of her ancestors.

Caroline Halliday
I am forty-three, white, a co-mother and a writer, politically involved in lesbian parenting and disability. For me, erotic writing is about mystery and pleasure, and far from pain or violence to the self or others. I have published poems, stories and articles, and am currently involved in editing two collections, on lesbian/children, and *A Different Kind of Death*, writings around death for lesbians and gay men. I am also writing this bio at the eleventh hour and learning to play canasta with my daughter.

Terri L Jewell
Terri Jewell, a fat Black dyke Libra from Kentucky, thirty-five, whose lover, a fat Black dyke Cancer from Indiana, thirty-nine, has three fingers that can lift Terri right off the bed. We are both poets/writers and very receptive to one another's passions.

Esther Y Kahn
Born London 1956 in unfortunate circumstances. Is a Diasporan Jew, and is currently looking for answers to the world going the wrong way. Wrote 'Suddenly One Summer' following a fascist attack on her home on the anniversary of Kristallnacht, 1989. (Kristallnacht is 'The Night of Broken Glass' when Nazis launched a major pogrom on German Jewish communities in 1939. This date, along with Hitler's birthday, is still 'celebrated' among European fascist communities.)

Sarah Kay
Sarah Kay divides her 'public' time between academia and the Labour Party. She is currently researching a new book entitled *Murder in the Council Chamber* which expresses the frustrations of a radical feminist working in the local state.

Daisy Kempe
Daisy Kempe has published short stories in British and Canadian literary magazines, and has published poems in *Naming the Waves*, edited by Christian McEwen, Virago, 1988, and in *The Virago Book of Love Poetry*, edited by Wendy Mulford, Virago, 1990. Under another name she is an established author of non-fiction women's studies. After mothering (one), step-parenting (three), and co-parenting (three), she now lives quietly with two cats in a small country village and writes.

L A Levy
L A Levy lives and works in London whilst dreaming of palm trees and wide open spaces. She is a speech therapist by day and an aspiring belly dancer by night. Her contribution was inspired by the resistance of women against terror, and those who struggle to create their own dreams.

Ingrid MacDonald
Ingrid MacDonald is a writer and visual artist living in Toronto. Other stories by Ingrid appear in the Canadian anthologies *Dykeversions*, 1986, and *Dykewords*, 1990. Ingrid is the production co-ordinator of *Rites* magazine for lesbian and gay liberation.

Marnia Montague
Nobody ever told me that fancying a wem was wrong. Nobody ever told me that fancying a mun was wrong. I developed in my own space. I wrote my first novel *Negret Mermet* when I was seventeen to twenty.

Spike Pittsberg
I am an old-gay type who has lived chunks of my life on three different continents. In addition to journalism, political analysis, and short fiction, I've been writing lewd dirt for some twenty years. Although I am not a 'materials' fetishist myself, I wrote this story in a decidedly unsuccessful attempt to seduce someone who is.

Susie Q
Susie Q — 36.26.35. Born ranking and rebellious, in the Dawning of the Age of Aquarius — Blessed Be! Q writes for all those girls who have considered suicide when the rainbow isn't enough. Tattoed and currently residing in Brixton, Q has been known to surface in *Shocking Pink, My Pony*, and *Light Horse*. Q sends a massive 'Yo!' to all the girls in the Loving Lesbian Nation aka The World.

Isabel Ross
Isabel Ross lives in rural Scotland. She is approaching fifty fast, and maturity rather more slowly. She hopes that her story will give solace, pleasure and encouragement to any open-minded woman who reads it.

Sapphire
Sapphire is the author of *Meditations on the Rainbow*. Her work has appeared in several anthologies including *Naming the Waves*, ed. Christian McEwan and *Women on Women*, eds. Joan Nestle and Naomi Holoch. A frequent contributor to lesbian and feminist publications in the US, Sapphire is currently working on an audio tape of her poetry, a novel and a collection of poetry and short fiction.

Anna Marie Smith
Anna Marie Smith — a Canadian living in London, engaged in doctoral study on 'post modern' political theory, but often distracted. She is a member of Femininsts Against Censorship, and has contributed to *On Our Backs* and the *Body Politic*.

Barbara Smith
My first lucky break — and it was luck — was to have a short story published in *Square Peg* in 1984, and I was over the moon. Since then my work has appeared in many lesbian and gay publications in the UK; most recently I have had stories published in the USA, in *On Our Backs, Out/Look* and *The Village Voice*. I am now working on my first novel. My advice to new writers is: Just go for it. If you're going to have a dream, you might as well make it a big one!

Jo Smith
Jo Smith is twenty years old and a triple Gemini. She comes from a small village in Leicestershire and she wants to be a film maker. She is a Nichiren Shoshu Buddhist. This is her first published work and it's a shame she can't show it to her mother.

Cherry Smyth
Cherry Smyth is a freelance writer. She has been published in *Serious Pleasure*, Sheba, 1989. She contributed to the *Feminist Guide to Cinema*, forthcoming from Virago, and has also a short story in *Seeing in the Dark*, to be published by Serpent's Tail, 1990. She ran the first university course on lesbians in film in 1990, and had an essay included in *Feminist Review, Perverse Politics: Lesbian Issues*, Spring 1990 on lesbian film and pornography.

Liann Snow
In youth: obsessive; angrily optimistic; indignantly homosexual; determinedly communicative of my own experience (through painting, poems, songs and prose). Now: a graduate; a gardener; a dyke-who-writes, and who draws and paints the Great Goddess (determinedly communicative of that experience).

Storme Webber
Writer, poet, singer, performer, visual artist. Originally from Seattle, USA, I have lived the past ten years in both San Francisco and New York City. I've performed and exhibited extensively on both coasts, and in London. Author of the book of poetry, prose and graphics, *Diaspora*, and an additional manuscript, *Wild Tales of a Renegade Half-Breed Bulldagger*. My artistic life aims are liberation and soulfullness; and to live the words of Assatta Shakur: 'Truth is my sword and love is my compass.' ACHÉ.

Hillary West
Black Country born, Yorkshire by naturalization. Single, Scorpio, twenty-eight; my interests are Barbara Pym and the subject of this poem.